A Lighthouse Snapshot

Jennifer Faye

Lazy Dazy Press

Copyright © 2024 by Jennifer F. Stroka

All rights reserved.

No portion of this book may be reproduced in any form without written permission from the publisher or author, except as permitted by U.S. copyright law.

Published by Lazy Dazy Press

Thanks & much appreciation to:

Editor: Lia Fairchild

Bluestar Island series:

Book 1: Love Blooms

Book 2: Harvest Dance

Book 3: A Lighthouse Café Christmas

Book 4: Rising Star

Book 5: Summer by the Beach

Book 6: Brass Anchor Inn

Book 7: Summer Refresh

Book 8: A Seaside Bookshop Christmas

Book 9: A Lighthouse Snapshot

Book 10: Inheriting Her Island House

About this book...

As tulips bloom and the sun warms the air, the Bluestar ferry delivers a special visitor to the island whose search for the past leads her directly in the path of her future.

With Spring Fling the next event on Bluestar's busy calendar, the residents decide to use it to play another round of matchmaking. Elaine "Lainey" Devereaux is led to the island by a cryptic entry in her late mother's journal. With the weight of grief driving Lainey onward, she searches for a long-buried secret, but before she can uncover the truth, there's a tragic accident.

Graphic artist Jack Turner is on top of the world as he anticipates a big promotion and a move to the Big Apple. He's minding his own business when the most beautiful woman rushes into the roadway, right in front of his cart. With no time to stop, the collision leaves both of them stunned. As circumstances conspire to draw them together, they soon find themselves helping each other to come to terms with the past while exploring an unexpected love.

Includes a recipe for Elegant Whoopie Pies!

Bluestar Island series:
Book 1 – Love Blooms (Hannah & Ethan)
Book 2 – Harvest Dance (Aster & Sam)
Book 3 – A Lighthouse Café Christmas (Darla & Will)
Book 4 – Rising Star (Emma & Noah)
Book 5 – Summer by the Beach (Summer & Greg)
Book 6 – Brass Anchor Inn (Josie & Lane)
Book 7 – Summer Refresh (Sara & Kent)
Book 8 – A Seaside Bookshop Christmas (Melinda & Liam)
Book 9 – A Lighthouse Snapshot (Lainey & Jack)
Book 10 – Inheriting Her Island House (Brianna & Grant)

Contents

Prologue		1
1.	Chapter One	5
2.	Chapter Two	16
3.	Chapter Three	26
4.	Chapter Four	35
5.	Chapter Five	49
6.	Chapter Six	56
7.	Chapter Seven	65
8.	Chapter Eight	79
9.	Chapter Nine	97
10.	Chapter Ten	108
11.	Chapter Eleven	116
12.	Chapter Twelve	128
13.	Chapter Thirteen	134
14.	Chapter Fourteen	145

15.	Chapter Fifteen	156
16.	Chapter Sixteen	168
17.	Chapter Seventeen	179
18.	Chapter Eighteen	190
19.	Chapter Nineteen	198
20.	Chapter Twenty	208
21.	Chapter Twenty-One	221
22.	Chapter Twenty-Two	232
23.	Chapter Twenty-Three	239
24.	Chapter Twenty-Four	247
25.	Chapter Twenty-Five	258
26.	Chapter Twenty-Six	264
	Epilogue	272
	The Elegant Bakery's Whoopie Pies	279
	Afterword	281
	About Author	282
	Also By	283

Prologue

Manhattan, New York

"There's a secret..." Her mother had shoved aside her oxygen mask. "I should have told you a long time ago. I..."

Her mother's last words echoed in Elaine "Lainey" Devereaux's mind. Her mother's voice had been raspy and frequently interrupted with harrowing bouts of coughing. "I love you... Before you were born, I..." There had been more coughing. "I took a very important road trip. I was searching for..."

That was it. That was all her mother had said before the coughing and wheezing had gotten so bad the medical staff had to intervene. Lainey had been forced from the room, never to hear her mother's voice again.

When she'd broached the subject with her father, he'd given her a blank stare. He told her he didn't know what her mother was referring to. Lainey didn't believe him, because her father had a tell—he would twist his wedding ring once and only once. It was as though he could tell he was doing it and would stop himself. So, what were her parents keeping from her?

Now with the funeral over, their Manhattan house was filled with people expressing their condolences. Lainey couldn't stomach one more word of sympathy. She couldn't shake another hand. And she didn't want any more hugs. None of it did anything to fill the gaping hole in her heart.

She missed her mother so much that words couldn't describe her grief. Not only had her mother been a great parent but as Lainey transformed into an adult, her mother had become a good friend. They'd shopped together. They'd lunched together. And most of all they'd talked about most anything—even about the guys Lainey dated.

Lainey quietly slipped to the steps. She made her way up a flight before she decided to keep going up to the third floor. She didn't have a destination in mind. She just wanted to get away from the sympathetic looks and empty words.

When she reached the landing, the tall double doors leading to her parents' bedroom loomed before her. She had knocked on that door and crossed over that threshold thousands of times throughout her life. In her mind she could still hear her mother's sweet voice calling out, "Come in."

Lainey's hand grasped the vintage French brass doorknob and swung the heavy door open. There was still a part of her expecting to find her mother curled up in the large armchair with floral upholstery that stood next to the fireplace. Lainey recalled how her mother would devour book after book in that very spot.

Now the chair stood empty with her mother's cream-colored throw folded and carefully hung over the back of the chair. The pain in Lainey's heart grew and threatened to send her into a fit of tears again. Her eyes burned, and her throat was raw from all of the crying she'd done in the last few days.

She turned her head, taking in her mother's side of the enormous four-poster bed. Next to it was her nightstand, where her mother had kept a framed photo of their little family—Lainey, her mother, and her father. As Lainey's gaze continued around the room, her attention came to rest on her mother's cedar chest, which was placed beneath a window.

Lainey moved to it. Her mother had told her that was where she'd kept her most treasured mementos. When her mother was alive, Lainey was never allowed to open the chest, but now Lainey longed for anything that would make her feel closer to her mother.

She knelt down and opened the lid. The scent of cedar enveloped her. She'd always enjoyed the smell. Her gaze focused on the contents of the chest. Right on top was Lainey's program from her law school graduation. On the other side was the birthday card she'd given her mother earlier that year. Lainey had no idea her mother kept so many things she'd given her.

Lainey shifted positions and crossed her legs. She worked her way through the mementos. They held so many good memories. There weren't just things from her but also cards and notes from her father. She didn't read those. And there was an old camera. She wondered if it still worked. She set it aside to investigate later.

She didn't know how much time had passed before she reached the bottom of the chest. It was there she found a brown leather journal. It looked weathered and old.

She couldn't remember ever seeing it before. She untied the string around it and flipped to the first page. The words *road trip* immediately caught her attention. Could this be the road trip her mother had started to tell her about in the hospital?

She rushed to put the other items back in the cedar chest just the way she'd found them. Then with the journal and camera in hand, she quietly made her way down a flight of stairs. Once in her bedroom, she curled up in a similar armchair, but instead of it being in front of a fireplace, hers was situated in front of the window. As the sun sank lower in the sky, she started to read...

Chapter One

Seven months later, Bluestar Island, Massachusetts

Were the answers she sought in front of her?

Lainey had to believe they were because she refused to stop searching until she uncovered the secret her mother never got to tell her.

After her mother's funeral, she was left with more questions than answers—like why no one from her mother's family came to the service. Her father had assured her that her mother was an only child and that her parents had passed long ago. Lainey couldn't stop thinking that there had to be cousins or old friends—someone to tell her the stories of her mother's past—someone to help keep her mother's memory alive.

She had so many questions. Her father refused to answer any of them. His stony silence drove a wedge between them. Now, they maintained a superficial relationship. He'd ask when she was coming back to work as a corporate attorney for his company. She'd answer that she didn't know. She had taken a leave of absence after her mother's funeral to do some traveling.

While traveling, she'd started blogging about the places she'd visited. Recently, she'd started selling some of the articles to a travel magazine. It was so different from her career as a contract attorney.

Lainey rode a ferry from Boston out to Bluestar Island. Strong wind and big swells in the ocean kept the ferry in constant motion. Her stomach moved up and down with the sea. She swallowed hard as she attempted to keep her nausea under control. Sailing wasn't for her.

Trying to distract herself, she turned until she could see her destination off in the distance. Since she'd never heard of Bluestar Island, she'd had to do some internet sleuthing before setting off on this adventure.

The photos that had been posted online had intrigued her. Since she was already in Boston and the island wasn't too far offshore, she decided this expedition was in order. She needed to find out if the *BS* she'd found in her mother's journal stood for Bluestar Island. If not, she'd keep searching until she found the answers she sought.

She once more adjusted the oversized black handbag on her shoulder. With her hand gripping the straps of the handbag so it wouldn't slip off again and her other hand gripping the handle of her luggage, she moved to the metal railing as the ferry neared the island. The salty sea air sent her brown hair whipping around. Her finger swept the strands off to the side and tucked them behind her ear, not that it would stay there long in this wind.

She lifted the camera, which hung around her neck. She'd been wearing it for so many months now that it felt as though it were a part of her, and she could hardly remember what it was like not to have a camera at the ready.

She snapped a picture of the water as the wind whipped it up into swell after swell. Her handbag slipped to the bend in her arm. She suppressed a sigh as she yanked it back on her shoulder. She continued to snap photos.

The late morning sunshine bounced off the surge of water, twinkling like a million diamonds scattered across the ocean. In that moment, Lainey felt the tension in her neck and shoulders ease. Even if this voyage was yet one more dead end on her extensive journey, it looked like a great place to spend the next couple of days. Perhaps it could be the focus of a new article for a magazine that had started to buy her travel spotlights.

She lowered the camera as Bluestar came into full view. As she once again adjusted her handbag on her shoulder, she continued to stare at the island. She didn't know what she'd been expecting but the island appeared to be quite large. Her research on the internet indicated the population was approximately ninety-five hundred full-time residents.

Overhead, the seagulls spread their wings wide as they coasted through the sky. They made it look so effortless and relaxing. She snapped their photo. The birds squawked as though welcoming her to the island.

The ferry slowed down as they entered the harbor. She noticed a big white sign with black and red print: *No wake zone. 5 mph speed limit.* They weren't the only ones to slow down. Speed boats and fishing boats also moved slowly across the water.

They were so close to docking now. Anticipation pulsed through her body. This past seven months she'd taken a leave of absence from her position as a corporate attorney within her father's business in order to follow in her mother's footsteps as laid out in her journal. Lainey had visited dozens of cities throughout the States from Charlotte, North Carolina, to Sante Fe, New Mexico, and onward to the Pacific Coast. She'd ended up making an entire loop around the continental United States.

She'd wanted to document her travels and so she'd started a blog. In the beginning, it'd just been for herself, but as she'd shared the posts on her social media, she'd quickly gained a following.

The amazing journey had been like a last gift from her mother. Of course, some of the places she had to guess at because her mother had used her shorthand for names and abbreviated them with initials. The mysterious initials only added to the adventure.

In the end, she'd had so much information for her travel blog that she was ahead of schedule by two months. It felt good to know that she had that many saved-up articles. And to her surprise, the traffic to her website was multiplying each month.

With the website being monetized, it meant she had a small but steady stream of income. It was modest compared to what she'd been earning as an attorney at the family business, but between the income and her savings, she'd been able to fund this journey. Through it all, she still had one question: Why had her mother ventured on this trip? What was she searching for? And what had she found?

Okay. So, maybe that was three questions instead of one. But she still hadn't learned about any secret. What was it? She wouldn't rest until she learned what was so important to her mother that it was her last words.

The Starfish Harbor came into view with its many piers. It was quite large with a lot of fishing boats in many different colors with their decks covered by nets and winches. Her gaze moved to the impressive sailboats with their masts climbing high into the blue sky.

She instinctively reached for the camera. She raised her shoulder to keep her heavy handbag from slipping down her arm. It wasn't comfortable, but she'd learned to cope with it.

Focus, adjust, and snap. It was like when she was behind a camera, she could see the world more clearly. As she focused on her surroundings, her thoughts were no longer centered around the loss of her mother or the nagging questions her father refused to answer.

As the ferry docked, she lowered her camera. She stared out at the busy harbor. People were rushing about. Fishermen, tourists, and locals were all in a hurry.

She grabbed her blue suitcase with a collection of stickers from the places she'd visited. She rolled it over to the line of passengers waiting to get off the ferry.

"Is this your first time to Bluestar?" An older woman with short snow-white hair sent her a warm smile.

Lainey took in the warmth in the woman's eyes and couldn't help but smile back. "Yes, it is. Do you live here?"

"I do. You'll love it here. My name's Birdie Neill." The woman looked expectantly at her.

Lainey had really hoped to keep her visit to the island quiet. Her father was powerful and newsworthy more often than not. She didn't doubt that he had contacts all over the place. It only took one person to recognize her name and connect it back to her headline-making father. If that happened, it would ruin her chance to quietly explore this island. Any chance she had to figure out what her mother meant to say would be snatched away when her father interfered.

Lainey could still feel the woman's curious gaze on her. "It's nice to meet you. I'm Lainey." She paused. What surname was she supposed to use? Certainly not Devereaux. She didn't want to be associated with her father and his business empire.

"Lainey Dell." It was her pen name.

"Well, Lainey Dell, do you have a place to stay on the island?"

Lainey shook her head. Not want to reveal too much about herself, she said, "I'm not sure I'm going to stay that long." When Birdie's gaze moved to her suitcase, Lainey said, "I'm touring New England. I saw a flyer about this place and thought I'd visit."

Birdie nodded in understanding. "You'll love it here. I came here many years ago for a visit, and my heart never left this island."

"I'm not thinking about moving."

"Neither was I at the time, but I fell in love with my husband as well as this island. And I've been happy here. If you give this island a chance, it can present you with your heart's true desire."

Lainey struggled not to keep her mouth from hanging open. It was almost as though Birdie had read her mind. But that wasn't possible, and she didn't believe in magic or whatever. Birdie was merely boasting about her home. That was all.

As Lainey observed the happiness that showed in the woman's eyes, she bit back her words of disagreement. Instead, she decided to ignore Birdie's last words. "You should be a spokesperson for the island. You make it sound like paradise."

A little color filled the woman's cheeks. "No one needs to hear me go on about the island's attributes when they can find out for themselves, just like you're about to do."

Lainey smiled at the woman, certain that if she were to live on the island that they would be fast friends. "I'm really looking forward to exploring this place."

Birdie's gaze moved to Lainey's suitcase. "If you don't want to drag that along with you, you can rent a locker in the ferry house. They have quite a few of them. And they are very secure."

She wasn't so sure about leaving her things in some office. She imagined some flimsy lockers like she'd had in high school. The thought didn't make her comfortable. She had some very valuable things in her luggage—including her mother's journal.

Still, she loved the idea of not having the suitcase in tow. Normally, she'd have left it in her hotel room, but this detour had been unexpected, and she didn't have reservations. It might be worth having a look around before she decided whether to stay the night or not.

Also, without her luggage in tow, it would be easier to take some more photos. If she didn't learn any information about her mother's family, she could use the pictures for a new travel article and sell the rest. Who knew the couple of photography classes she'd taken in college would come in so handy now?

While they slowly moved toward the ramp leading to the dock, Birdie chatted about the island. She told Lainey to stop by the Lighthouse Café for lunch and a number of other places. Lainey tried to memorize the names, but there were so many it was impossible to remember them all. There was more to do on the island than she'd been expecting.

On the dock, she thanked Birdie before they went their separate ways. "I appreciate all of the information you shared with me. I'll definitely swing by the Lighthouse Café for lunch."

"You won't be disappointed." Birdie glanced around. "There's my ride. I need to be going. I hope we run into each other again."

Lainey was surprised by how much she liked that idea, but she told herself at the beginning of this journey not to get too attached to any place or anyone. She couldn't stay. She had to keep moving around until she found the truth. It was out there just waiting for her to uncover it.

"I would like that," Lainey said, "but I don't think I'll be here very long."

When Birdie reached out to give her a hug, Lainey hugged her back. She hadn't hugged anyone since her mother's funeral. Her father wasn't a hugger, and she'd broken up with the guy she'd been seeing for a couple of months before her mother's passing.

What was it about Birdie that put her at ease? She had a feeling if she were to move to Bluestar that she would adopt Birdie as a surrogate grandmother.

After they parted, Lainey made her way to the Bluestar Ferry office. The place was certainly nothing fancy. The walls were white with lots of posters and circulars about places of interest on the island as well as those in Boston.

She moved toward the long wooden counter that spanned the width of the building. There were a few people ahead of her in line. Young and old alike stood with their luggage or a duffle bag. It would appear it was common for people to come here to store those things. It made her feel a little better about leaving her belongings.

A middle-aged man with close-cropped gray hair and a woman about the same age with her brown hair pulled back in a bun worked behind the counter. Lainey observed the man behind the counter open a small gate to allow a young man back into the locker area. The young man was escorted to the rows of gray lockers. This was nothing like she'd imagined. It was so much better. Birdie hadn't led her wrong.

When it was her turn at the counter, she filled out a short form, put the charge for the locker on her credit card, and was escorted to the back of the building. The area was well lit. She was impressed with the size of the compartment. She easily placed her suitcase in the locker.

The handbag slipped down her arm for the umpteenth time that day. The designer handbag had been her mother's. Upon her mother's death, her father had let Lainey pick through her mother's belongings and take what she wanted—the handbag had been one of those things.

She remembered her mother carrying it everywhere with her. It was old but had been lovingly cared for. When Lainey looked at it, she could still picture her mother with the handbag on her shoulder and a smile on her face. It seemed only fitting that she should take it on this journey. She just hadn't thought about how annoying it would be when she was trying to take photographs.

Perhaps it was time they took a break from each other. Her shoulder could certainly use a respite. Before she could change her mind, she grabbed some cash and then stuffed the bag on top of her suitcase.

She glanced over at the older woman who had escorted her to the locker area. "You're certain that everything will be secure?"

"Yes, ma'am. Everyone is escorted back here, and they must provide a picture ID before being given access to the locker. We've never once had anything stolen."

Speaking of photo ID, she reached into the bag and grabbed hers. She shoved it into her pocket along with the cash. It wasn't like she'd be gone long. With her camera around her neck, she made her way into town.

Her next surprise was finding out that the island didn't allow automobiles. She ended up taking a Bluestar Taxi Cart. Deciding she was hungry, she made her first stop the Lighthouse Café. She hoped the food was as good as Birdie had said.

Chapter Two

How much longer was this going to take?

Jack Turner set down his end of a heavy black leather couch in the large display window of his family's furniture business. The store had changed a lot over the years.

He turned around and took in the large showroom. It was twice the size it was when he was a kid. A wall had been taken down, turning part of their storage area into an expanded showroom floor. It had been his older brother's idea.

As Jack looked around the place, he remembered how it had looked once upon a time. His mind conjured up the memories of the past. It was like the clock had been rolled back, and he was once more a teenager, working in his family's furniture store.

All six Turner kids had worked in the store at one point in their lives. Their father said it taught them responsibility and a lesson in hard work. They did get paid for their time, which most of them promptly spent at Whippy Dips, Island Flicks Theatre, or the Pedal On Bike Shop.

Those memories seemed so far away. A lot had changed since those days for his whole family. And now Kent was running the family business. Everything had worked out like it should have—except for him.

Jack thought by now that he'd be happily married with a family of his own. Well, he'd gotten married, but it wasn't long after that everything had fallen apart. There was an ache in his heart that would never go away.

"Hey!" Kent frowned at him.

Jack got the feeling his brother had been speaking to him, but he had no clue what he'd said. "What?"

"What's the matter with you?" Kent narrowed his gaze on him.

"I don't know what you're talking about."

"The past few months, you haven't been yourself. You're quieter. And it's like something is bothering you."

Realizing he'd let thoughts of his past distract him, he gave himself a mental shake. "I'm just distracted with work. I'm working on a presentation, and I'm hoping it'll gain me a promotion."

"Oh. I see." Kent sent him a relieved look. "Congratulations."

"Hey, man. It's way too soon for that word. I don't need you to jinx me."

"Sorry. I take it back. Am I allowed to wish you luck?"

Jack shrugged. "I suppose that wouldn't hurt."

"Good. Now back to work. This isn't the right spot for the couch." Kent glanced around the display area. "Move it back a foot."

Jack didn't want to lift any more heavy furniture. This wasn't his job. Still, his brother didn't ask for help very often, so he bent over and once more picked up the couch. He moved his end of the couch where he thought his brother wanted it.

"That looks good." Kent turned and leaned against the couch with a sigh.

"If I knew you were going to make me work this hard, I would have had you put me on the payroll."

Kent let out a laugh as he shook his head. "You don't need anything I could offer. You have a really good job with Sharps Unlimited."

Jack nodded his head. "Guilty as charged. And I should be working on that job right now instead of helping you move furniture around. Don't you have employees to help you with this stuff?"

"Normally I do, but two are out sick and another is on vacation."

Jack nodded in understanding. "And Mom and Dad are in Maine visiting Aunt Susan and Uncle Jim. Maybe you need to hire more help."

"We just hired Aunt Carol. And it's taking more money to get the refresh business off the ground than I had anticipated."

"I'm sure that it's going to take off. Everyone loved what you did at the Brass Anchor Inn, and now at the Seaside Bookshop. People are still talking about the amazing transformations."

"I just need the projects to move quicker." He lowered his voice. "Did you know that our aunt is a perfectionist?"

Jack shook his head. "I didn't have a clue."

"Each project is taking twice as long as it needs to."

"I don't know what to tell you. Have you tried talking to her?"

Kent dramatically rolled his eyes. "It didn't go very well. She asked me if I wanted the project done correctly or quickly. I felt like there wasn't a correct answer. I tried to explain to her that we needed to complete each refresh project at a faster pace, but she said this was more than just redecorating and that there was no rushing an artist. An artist?"

Jack laughed. "It appears you've created a temperamental artist."

"And here I thought I was hiring our aunt to do some small cosmetic makeovers."

Ding.

Jack reached for his phone. There was a reminder that he had an important business meeting in a half hour. And he couldn't miss it. He was told by his boss that it was mandatory.

Jack slipped his phone back into his pocket. "I've got to get going. I have a meeting."

"Wait. I just need help with one more thing."

Jack arched an eyebrow. "That's what you said two pieces of furniture ago."

"I'm serious this time. I need to bring one of the recliners out here for the window display."

"And it can't wait?"

"No. I need to arrange it for the sale."

"Of course, you do." Jack sighed. "Well, come on. I have to hurry."

They moved to the storage room, and it took Kent a moment to locate the navy-blue recliner. Once he found it, Jack knew why he needed help moving it. That thing was heavy—heavier than the couch they had just moved to the showroom window. How was that possible?

He glanced up at the big black-and-white wall clock. If he didn't leave now, he was going to be late. And yet he couldn't just bail on his brother.

The island was even prettier than the photos.

Once away from Starfish Harbor, Lainey noticed all of the colorful Cape Cod–style houses as well as unique businesses. She didn't spot one chain store. *Interesting.* She couldn't wait to go exploring. This place was a goldmine of travel articles just waiting to be written.

After having problems taking photos in the bouncy cart, she had the Bluestar Taxi Cart drop her off on the side of a random road. She decided she wanted to walk the rest of the way to the Lighthouse Café. It would give her a chance to take some photos. And there was plenty to photograph from the picturesque streets with quaint shops to the view of the ocean.

When she wasn't snapping photos, her mother's old camera hung around her neck. She wondered if her mother had once upon a time loved photography. She'd never mentioned it to her. Maybe it was just a passing interest when her mother was young. She wished she could ask her—there were so many things she wanted to ask her.

Sure she could use her digital camera, but it wasn't quite the same. Maybe it was because she'd hoped this journey would bring her closer to her mother because she missed her—she missed her so much.

A wave of grief came out of nowhere. It rolled through her, knocking the breath from her lungs and leaving behind a ragged pain. She'd thought the deep sadness and longing to see her mother again would fade with time. It hadn't. She was slowly learning to live with the loss.

"I love you," a young man said behind her.

"I love you more," a female voice replied.

"No. I love you more."

The sound of their steps was gaining on Lainey. She stepped off to the side to let them pass. She watched as the young couple passed by her. They were hand-in-hand with love written all over their faces.

"I love you the most-est," the young woman said proudly.

"That's not a word," the man fired back.

"It is now. I win." The woman grinned at the guy.

Lainey welcomed the distraction. It reminded her that there was more to this world than death.

There were experiences in between birth and death that made life worth living. And this was one of them.

She continued walking behind the couple, who were slowly widening the space between her and them. She was drawn in by the very obvious love between these two. It gave Lainey hope that there was a happily-ever-after out there for her too. Not that she was looking for a guy. She didn't have time to get distracted. Because she wasn't stopping her journey until she learned the secret her mother alluded to.

They stopped walking.

"No. I win." The guy turned to the woman and withdrew a black ring box from his pocket.

The woman's eyes widened. She audibly gasped or had that been Lainey? She'd never seen anyone do a proposal right in front of her. It was almost like her mother was sending her a sign from the other side—that she wasn't supposed to give up on the good things in life.

The young woman pressed a hand to her mouth. The guy dropped to one knee. He opened the box and held it up to her.

Lainey stopped. Her mouth gaped as this most special moment unfolded right in front of her. It pumped a little joy into her aching heart. And for that moment, she wasn't thinking about how life had let her down—how her parents had let her down.

She wasn't the only one to be caught up in the moment. People on both sides of the street stopped to watch the proposal. How could anyone pass by this magical moment?

The man knelt there on the sidewalk, holding up the ring, which sparkled in the sunlight. "Melinda Coleman, I have loved you for what feels like forever and in other ways it feels like our story has just begun. You bring out the best in me and make me want to strive to be a better man." As the man spoke, the woman smiled as happy tears streamed down her cheeks. "Life is an adventure, and I'm hoping you'll go on that adventure with me. Will you marry me?"

There was a slight pause. Lainey's breath caught in her lungs. Surely the woman was going to say yes. As the moment stretched on, Lainey began to worry. She was going to say yes, wasn't she?

Lainey had never seen these people before, and suddenly, she was so invested in this scene having its happily-ever-after. She needed the woman to accept—she needed to believe that there was a deep and abiding love out there for everyone. She needed to know that someday she might be able to get past this profound loss and feel the warmth of an all-encompassing love. She wanted to be able to feel the sort of happiness that started in her heart and worked its way to her smile.

Lainey's full attention was focused on this couple. She was utterly captivated by the love that showed in the man's eyes as the woman became overcome with emotion.

"Yes." The woman nodded and cried...all the while smiling. "Yes, I will."

The man removed the ring from the box and slipped it onto his bride-to-be's finger.

In that moment Lainey realized she could contribute something to this moment. "Wait!"

Both heads turned in her direction, confusion written all over their faces. The man was the first to speak. "What do you want?"

With the guy still on bended knee, Lainey asked, "Can I take your photo?" When the guy went to straighten, Lainey said, "Don't move. It's a perfect shot with you right there."

He remained kneeling as he glanced up at his bride. The woman shrugged. It was obvious she'd caught them off guard. It wasn't the first time she'd surprised people with her request to take their photo.

"I'll make sure you get a copy," she said.

"Why do you want our photo?" the guy asked.

"Because it's small-town love. It's perfect. People will love the story—your story." She stopped herself, knowing she was getting ahead of herself. "My name's Lainey, um, Dell." She spoke quickly as though worried about getting cut off before she could get it all out there. "I'm a travel blogger, and this would be great for a story. But even if you don't want your story published, I'd still be willing to take the photo for you."

"It's okay with me." The guy glanced at his future wife. "What do you think?"

The woman smiled as she nodded.

"Go ahead," he said to Lainey. "Do you want me to stay here?"

"Yes." She sensed he wasn't comfortable. She had to hurry and take the shot, but she also knew it had to be a perfect photograph so they would have something special to look back on. She was much too close. When she went to step back, she found a crowd had formed behind her. She moved toward the quiet road. "Can you take her hand in yours and stare up at her?"

The man did as she asked. The love was evident in the way they stared deeply into each other's eyes. Lainey snapped a photo. And another from a different angle.

It'd be great to get a bit more of the background. When the man once more went to stand, Lainey said, "Stay right there. I want to take one more photo. I just need to back up..."

She focused her attention on the view through the camera lens as she kept stepping back, needing to pick up more of the Lighthouse Café's white bricks behind them...

Thunk!

Chapter Three

He couldn't be late.

Jack rushed home. He had an important Zoom meeting with his group from Sharps Unlimited. They mostly worked remotely. Once a month, he was required to travel into Manhattan to work in the office for a couple of days. Once in a while, his presence in New York was longer, but most of the time he was able to work remotely from Bluestar Island. He loved the freedom of being able to work in shorts, choosing the hours he worked, and so many other privileges.

Jack enjoyed a quiet, regulated life until his family descended upon him. He was the only one of the six Turner siblings that was ever on time for anything—and by on time he meant at least fifteen minutes early.

Jack sat back in his dark blue golf cart, the island's primary source of transportation. His cousin Summer Turner waved to him as he made his way through town. Jack waved back. Lily Adams also waved. Jack waved again. This happened repeatedly.

And then Mary Miller flagged him down. The woman was in her sixties and very active in the town's gossip mill. She wore a serious look on her round face, and he worried something was wrong.

When he pulled the cart to a stop, she rushed up to him. "I talked to Melinda Coleman, and she said you're bringing chocolate chip cookies to the party tomorrow night. Is that right?"

This was important enough to flag him down? He stifled a sigh. Tomorrow was a surprise birthday party for Horace Blackwell. For all of Jack's life, Horace had been known as the town Scrooge, but this past Christmas, there had been a miraculous change in the man. Maybe it was almost dying that changed him. Then again, maybe it was Melinda's big heart that had Horace transforming into a genuinely friendly person. Or maybe it was a combination of those things as well as the Christmas spirit. Jack didn't think he'd ever know the true reason.

It didn't matter. Melinda wasn't letting up on her project to reintroduce Horace to society. She'd planned a smallish birthday party for him that evening at the bookstore, and somehow Jack had gotten roped into not only attending but bringing cookies. He made a mental note to swing by the Elegant Bakery to pick up a dozen cookies. They had the finest baked goods on the island.

"Yes," he said. "I'm bringing cookies."

Her eyes lit up. "Oh, good. And would you happen to be bringing a date?"

Now he knew what had been the emergency. Mary was attempting to set him up. "No—"

Before he could get out another word, she said, "My niece is on the island for a visit. She's your age, and she's so beautiful. I just know you two would get along famously."

"I'm sorry. I'd really like to talk more, but I'm late for a meeting."

"Oh. Okay. I just wanted to tell you about Janet. She'd be perfect for you. I know you're going to love her."

He inwardly groaned. "I've really got to go."

She nodded in understanding as she continued to talk. "We'll see you at the party. I'll tell Janet you're anxious to meet her. Remember, the party is a secret." She lifted a finger to her lips. "So shh..."

Considering he wasn't going around talking about the surprise party, he didn't think he was the problem. Biting back his words, he smiled and then tramped the accelerator.

He glanced at his watch. *Seriously*? He had four minutes until the start of the meeting. He pressed harder on the accelerator. Thankfully, it was finally April, and it was a warm spring. It was like a bonus because the locals got to enjoy the nice weather before the tourists descended upon the island. It also meant a lot less congestion in the center of town.

He glanced down at the speedometer. Each cart on the island was required to have a speedometer installed because in recent years the town council had voted to post speed limits throughout the town. As tourism grew, so did the number of incidents with carts and people. Many years ago that hadn't been the case. After all, they were just golf carts, locals would say. But the accidents started to pile up, and the town council decided that safety came first.

When he glanced down at the speedometer, he found he was fifteen miles over the posted limit. What were the chances he'd get caught? And yes, there was a chance because just recently the town had invested in a speed radar gun. But seriously, there was only one law enforcement officer working at a time, and he couldn't be everywhere.

As Jack cruised through town, he was relieved to find it not very busy, so there were fewer pedestrians to contend with and no traffic to speak of. Still, he wasn't one for breaking the rules. Jack let up on the accelerator.

He again glanced down at the speedometer and saw the gauge lowering to a more reasonable speed. When he raised his gaze, he saw a young woman stepping into the roadway. Right in front of him. He tramped the brakes. His heart slammed into the back of his throat.

It all happened in the blink of an eye. There was no time to call out. No time to swerve.

The woman kept coming.

The cart kept moving forward.

Thunk!

Jack watched in horror as the woman bounced off the front of his cart. Something in her hand flew. She fell to the asphalt in front of his now-stopped cart.

No. No. No. This can't be happening.

A horrified gasp echoed over the crowd.

For an instant, Jack was thrown back in time. It had been a dark, rainy night. Everything had been perfect, until it suddenly wasn't.

There had been puddling on the roadway. One moment the car was rolling over the asphalt, and the next moment they were hydroplaning.

"Jack!" His brother's voice drew Jack to the present. "Jack, are you all right?"

He blinked and looked at the worried look on Liam's face. He swallowed hard. "Yes."

Jack turned off his cart and jumped out. His firefighter training kicked in as he moved to the woman's side. She lay there on the roadway with her eyes closed, as though she were napping. But the trickle of blood streaking down her forehead drove home the seriousness of the situation.

He'd been a firefighter since he graduated high school. His other brothers Liam and Kent were part of the fire department too. His oldest brother, Grant, used to be a firefighter until he went away to medical school. It was a duty passed down through his family from generation to generation.

Jack immediately checked for a pulse. She had one. It was strong and steady. That was a huge relief. If only she would open her eyes.

"What have you done?" a voice called out in the crowd.

Another voice said, "Nine-one-one has been called."

Jack glanced over his shoulder to find his brother Liam standing there next to his girlfriend, Melinda. "I... I didn't see her. She just stepped out in front of me."

A siren sounded as a cart pulled up. Jack turned to see the sheriff's tan and green cart with a red can light on top. Even though the officer wore sunglasses, Jack could see the frown written all over the man's face. It was like he was blaming him for this accident, and he didn't even know the facts. Or possibly it was Jack's own guilt that he was projecting onto Sheriff Connor Harrison.

The sheriff's gaze took in the scene and without asking a question, he reached for the mic and radioed dispatch for additional help. Almost immediately, the fire whistle began to blow.

Jack willed her to open her eyes.

The sheriff knelt down next to Jack. "How is she?"

Jack tore his gaze from the mystery woman to the sheriff. "She's been like this since she went down."

"What happened?" The sheriff propped his sunglasses on the top of his head as he pulled out a pen and notepad.

"I hit her." Jack's admission was quick.

"It was an accident," Liam said.

"You saw the accident?" The sheriff directed his question directly to Jack's brother.

Liam hesitated and then nodded.

"I'll need to speak to you and anyone else who saw what happened." His gaze moved around to the growing crowd of rubberneckers.

The sheriff started taking interviews for his accident report. Meanwhile, Jack and Liam stayed by the woman's side as they waited for the ambulance. *What is taking it so long?*

Usually, Jack was on the other side of those calls. He knew that for first responders, time flew by as they rushed to an accident scene. But being on the other end of the call, he realized how each minute felt as though it dragged out. Seconds turned to minutes.

His brother took him by the arm to pull him aside. Jack didn't budge.

"I'm not moving until the paramedics get here."

Liam remained quiet as he stood by his side.

Jack couldn't take his eyes off the beautiful woman as she lay in the roadway like some sort of Sleeping Beauty. He prayed she'd open her eyes. She just had to be all right.

As if in answer to his silent prayer, her brown eyes with golden flecks fluttered open. She stared directly at him. Her eyes were clouded with confusion and fear.

"You're all right." He kept his voice calm just like he'd done so many other times at accident scenes.

"Wha... What happened?" Her voice was faint as she raised her free hand to her head.

"I'm so sorry. I didn't see you. And suddenly, you were in front of my cart."

Her eyes widened. "You hit me?"

He nodded his head. "I'm really sorry. But you're going to be all right."

At last, another siren wailed. It grew closer until the sea of people parted to let the ambulance through. She looked at him like she wanted to say something more, but before she could formulate what she wanted to say, the paramedics approached them.

"You're going to be fine." His gaze met hers. "These people are going to help you."

And then he was pulled away from the woman's side as the paramedics moved in. She held a hand to her head, as though it were hurting her. As the medics started their examination, Jack willed her to be all right.

If he hadn't stopped to help Kent, he would have been at home doing his video meeting, and none of this would have happened. The woman would be fine, and he wouldn't be pacing impatiently as his buddies from the fire department worked on the patient.

The sheriff made his way over to him. The look on the man's face was serious. "Jack, do you know that you were speeding?"

"I..." He thought back but couldn't recall the exact speed. But he had been slowing down. Surely he couldn't have been going that fast.

"Would it surprise you to know that I have you clocked going ten miles over the speed limit?"

While the sheriff explained about the new radar equipment the island had purchased, Jack's full attention was on the young woman. For the first time since this whole horrible debacle, he was able to take a full breath. It looked like she was going to be all right. *Thank goodness.*

"I need to go." Jack wanted to apologize to the young woman.

"Not so fast." The sheriff stepped in his way. "I'm writing you up for speeding."

Jack's gaze swung around to face the sheriff. "You're giving me a ticket?"

"You're lucky that's all I'm doing. So far every witness has stated that she rushed into the roadway, and there was no time for you to stop."

Jack took in the sheriff's serious expression: his brows drawn together into a firm line, the hard set of his clean-shaven jaw, and the purse of his lips. Jack couldn't believe this was happening. He'd made it the whole way through his youth without getting into any serious trouble. And now that he was a responsible adult, he was about to get his first ticket.

However, he'd pay ten tickets if it would mean the young woman was all right. Guilt weighed heavy on his shoulders.

Chapter Four

Her head hurt. A lot.

Lainey slowly pried her eyes open. The brightness of the sun blinded her. She closed them again. Why was she staring up at the sun?

It took her a moment to realize she was lying on the ground. She opened her eyes again, averting them from the ball of fire in the sky. Instead, her gaze met a bunch of worried strangers staring down at her. This wasn't good. She didn't like to be the center of attention. Not at all.

Even though she was the daughter of Lance Devereaux, business mogul and entrepreneur as well as owner of LMD Inc., she'd always ducked the cameras. As she grew up, her father had garnered the spotlight for his savvy business acquisitions and his philanthropy. Her father had always been at ease in front of the camera, while she had been the exact opposite.

Where was she? She felt a hard surface beneath her hands. On the sidewalk? No. She was on the road. When she went to turn her head, she couldn't. There was something on her neck. She reached for the most uncomfortable thing to take it off.

"Relax," a woman said in a friendly voice. "You've been in an accident."

"Where am I?"

"You're on Bluestar Island."

Bluestar Island? She'd never heard of it. What was she doing there? She had so many questions and no answers.

"We're going to take you to the medical center to be examined."

"No. I don't need to go."

Firm hands held her in place.

"You really need to be checked by a doctor. It was quite a hit you took to your head, and you were out for a bit."

Lainey didn't know what the woman meant, but the pounding in her head took the fight out of her. Maybe this was more serious than she'd originally thought. As she relaxed, they moved her to a stretcher.

What exactly had happened? She couldn't remember. There was this big black hole in her memory. The more she struggled to find the answers, the more they eluded her.

Her heart beat faster. What was wrong with her? Worried that she'd totally lost her memory, she searched for what she did know. She recalled her real name: Elaine Devereaux and her pen name Lainey Dell.

Wait. If she could remember all of that, it must mean she hadn't lost her memory. She breathed out a pent-up breath. As they transported her a short distance and wheeled her into some sort of medical facility, she tried to remember what had happened to her, but it felt like her pounding headache was standing between her and those memories. The last thing she could recall was arriving in Boston, Massachusetts.

She asked a passing nurse where exactly she was and found out she was in a medical center on Bluestar Island. What was she doing there? Her thoughts were fuzzy. No matter how hard she tried, she couldn't remember. She inwardly groaned. This was so frustrating.

During the next couple of hours, she was poked and prodded. Thankfully, they'd given her some painkillers. It was taking the edge off of her headache.

"Hi. Do you have a moment to talk?"

When she turned her head, she saw a tall man in a sheriff's uniform. Even though he was good-looking in a strong, authoritative way, he wasn't nearly as handsome as the mystery man from the accident scene.

"Did you find my belongings?" She willed him to say yes.

"I'm sorry. We didn't see anything. What exactly are you missing?"

She described her mother's black bag, which she carried everywhere with her, and her luggage with a million stickers. It would be hard to miss. She just didn't understand what had happened to everything. She supposed there was a chance that during the confusion of the accident that someone might have walked off with them. She hoped not.

"I'll make sure to keep an eye out for them." He jotted something in his notebook. "Can you tell me your version of the accident?"

She shook her head, which made it hurt worse, so she stopped. "I can't remember."

The sheriff frowned. "You can't remember anything at all?"

"I'm having problems remembering the last couple of days. The doctor said those memories might come back to me, but they might be lost for good."

"I'm sorry to hear that." He sighed. "Well, the statements I have so far say that you stepped out into the roadway without looking, and that the incident was an accident. Do you disagree with this conclusion?"

She shrugged. "I don't know. I can't remember."

The sheriff nodded. "I understand." He reached into his shirt pocket and withdrew a business card. "This is my card. If you remember anything, call me."

She accepted the card. The name on it was Sheriff Harrison. "I'll let you know if my memory comes back to me."

"And I will let you know if your belongings turn up. Get some rest. I hope you feel better."

"Thank you."

After the sheriff left, she leaned her head back against the pillow. Her head ached. Maybe if the pain stopped, she'd be able to fill in the holes in her memory. She closed her eyes. She just needed to rest, and hopefully, when she opened her eyes again, the world will have righted itself.

She didn't know how long she'd lain there before she heard a voice call out her name. Her eyes fluttered open. There was the distinct possibility she'd dozed off for a moment. Sadly, it hadn't made her headache go away.

A young nurse approached the end of her bed. "How are you doing?"

Lainey wasn't sure how she was supposed to respond. "Okay. I guess." She didn't like hospitals. She didn't have good memories of them. "How soon can I get out of here?"

"That's up to the doctor. But in the meantime, I have someone here to see you."

"Is it the sheriff again? I told him all I know about the accident, which wasn't much."

"No. It's someone else."

"Someone else?" She couldn't imagine whom it might be. Had she forgotten she was traveling with someone? But who?

As Lainey considered what to do, the nurse looked a bit impatient. "I can send him away."

With her memory a bit fuzzy, she thought it might be best to see this person. Maybe they could fill in the gaps in her recollections. "No. I'll see him."

She immediately lifted her hands to run them over her hair, but an IV line in the back of her hand, a pulse oximeter on her pointer finger, and a blood pressure cuff impeded her movement. The blood pressure cuff began to fill with air. She lowered her arm. There was no way she could raise her arm while that was going on and so, she gave up. It wasn't like it mattered what she looked like. She didn't know this person and most likely wouldn't see them again.

The cuff around her arm felt plenty tight to her, and yet it continued to squeeze her arm. Her back teeth ground together. *It hurts*! Not like it was a little uncomfortable; no, this felt as though it were cutting off all blood flow. Her hand began to tingle. How could a few seconds of pain feel like it was going on forever?

Just then she heard footsteps. She didn't know who she expected to find standing a few feet away from the end of her bed, but it certainly wasn't the handsome man staring at her with the most mesmerizing dark brown eyes. She was so caught off guard by his presence it distracted her from the blood pressure cuff.

As the cuff began to relieve the pressure, she wondered if she'd met the man before the accident. Of course, she must have. Otherwise, what was he doing here?

She still hadn't remembered what she was doing in Bluestar. She'd never heard of this place. She had no idea why she would have traveled to this island. Was it part of her search for her mother's secret? Or was it merely an assignment for the magazine that she occasionally wrote travel pieces for?

She wondered if the handsome man standing before her would know the answers. As her gaze took in his short dark brown hair with its strands scattered as though the breeze had combed through it, her fingers tingled with the desire to reach out and fix it for him. Not that she would ever do that. As far as her faulty memory was concerned, he was a total stranger. Or was he?

Heat rushed to her cheeks as she realized she'd been staring at him. She glanced away. Her attention landed on the monitor next to the bed with the numbers flashing at her. Was her heart rate elevated? Yes. Definitely.

The man shifted his weight from one foot to the other as he shoved his hands into the pockets of his dark jeans. It appeared she wasn't the only one who was uncomfortable. His gaze lowered to the white tile floor. She found it strange he didn't speak first.

She swallowed hard, hoping when she spoke that her voice sounded normal. "Did you want to see me?"

His gaze lifted to meet hers. "I... I wanted to make sure you were okay."

She nodded. The movement made her headache worse, so she stopped. "I should be. I'm just waiting for the doctor to discharge me." She had the distinct feeling she should know him. "Do I know you?"

His dark brows rose. "Uh... No." The corners of his lips lifted into a barely-there smile. "I'm Jack Turner."

Was that a dimple in his cheek? She wanted to say something that would make him smile even more, but nothing came to mind. Instead, she said, "Hi, Jack. I'm Lainey."

Before their conversation could progress any further, the doctor approached her. She noticed that he held a clipboard with papers attached. She didn't have a lot of experience with hospitals, but she'd thought they'd all gone digital by now. Apparently this little island was behind the times. It was that or she'd gone back in time. The thought of her becoming a time traveler created a bubble of laughter in the back of her throat. But a quick look at the serious expression on the doctor's face had her subduing the laugh. The last thing she needed was to give the doctor any reason to keep her here longer than necessary.

His gray hair was trimmed short and a bit mussed up, as though he'd been rubbing his head while in deep thought. He had a pair of black-rimmed reading glasses perched atop his head. The worry lines bracketing his eyes and mouth held her attention.

When the doctor's gaze landed on her visitor at the end of her bed, his eyes momentarily widened. "Jack, I didn't expect to find you here."

"Hey, Doc. It's good to see you. I just wanted to make sure Lainey was all right." Jack turned back to her. "Doc Mullins will take good care of you. He's the island's only full-time doctor."

"I was just about to go over her results with her. If you'll excuse us."

"Uh…" Jack hesitated as though he had more to say to her. "Sure. I'll be in the waiting area."

Once he was gone, the doctor lowered his reading glasses and read her chart. "You don't have any broken bones, but you have a concussion."

She might not have broken any bones, but her entire body hurt. It felt as though each part of her was either scraped or bruised.

The older man lifted his glasses, resting them atop his head as his gaze met hers. "How does your head feel?"

She thought of lying because she so desperately wanted out of here, but she knew he would have seen on her chart that she'd requested painkillers. With a resigned sigh, she said, "It still hurts."

He nodded as though expecting that answer. "I'm concerned about your headache and the lapses in your memory. I would like to transfer you to a hospital on the mainland."

"What?" This was the last thing she expected or wanted. "No. I'm fine."

He continued talking as though she hadn't said anything. "They have more sophisticated equipment on the mainland, and I am recommending a CAT scan."

She shook her head, ignoring the pain that it created. "No. I don't need that."

The doctor's bushy brows drew together. "Your head injury could be serious."

The serious part was the way the walls of this place felt as though they were closing in on her. Memories of her mother dying in one were still too fresh in her mind. Her chest felt as though a vice had been placed around it, and someone was tightening it little by little. She couldn't stay here or at another hospital. It simply wasn't going to happen.

"I don't care." She struggled to keep the panic out of her voice. "I need out of here."

"You know you aren't the first person to feel that way about being in the hospital."

"It's just that I don't have good memories."

The doctor nodded in understanding. "So, you're refusing further medical care?"

This time she didn't move her head. "Yes, I am."

"Is there anything I can say to change your mind?" The doctor's unwavering gaze implored her to listen to his medical recommendation.

"No. I'll be fine." She figured if she said it enough times, it would be true.

He frowned. "I don't like this, but I can't force you to go to the other hospital." His gaze narrowed. "However, I want to see you tomorrow." His tone was firm. "This is non-negotiable."

She figured she'd pushed her luck as far as she could at this point. And she really didn't want anything to be wrong. Hopefully, by tomorrow her headache will have subsided, and her memory wouldn't be like Swiss cheese.

"Fine. Am I good to go?"

"Not so fast. I don't want you to be alone tonight. Do you have family or friends you can stay with?"

She didn't have either of those things on this island. The doctor looked at her expectantly. She knew if she didn't give him the name of someone, that he'd go back to insisting she remain here overnight. And there was no way she could relax in this bright white, antiseptic-smelling, sterile place. She would lie there and remember her mother in the hospital. It had been the worst time of her life.

"I can stay with Jack." She had absolutely no idea who Jack was. She had absolutely no idea who Jack was or if he was a nice guy. He did seem like it, though, to check on her. She didn't even know if he had a significant other.

But none of that mattered. All she had to do was get out of there. She'd figure out where she was going to stay after that. And it wouldn't be with Jack. She could take care of herself.

The doctor nodded as he made a note in her chart. "Jack's a good guy, and he's also a first responder, so you'll be in good hands, although not as good as being in the hospital…"

Her discharge wasn't immediate. There was paperwork to fill out. When she was finally on her way, she turned her attention to locating her purse and luggage. With her memory being faulty, she didn't know where to begin to look for them. The only thing she did have was her phone. She withdrew it from her back pocket. The screen was smashed and appeared to be dead. She inwardly groaned and added it to her list of problems she needed to deal with.

When she reached the waiting area, her head was still bothering her. Thanks to the medicine, it was a dull ache instead of a pounding headache. All she wanted to do was lie down in the dark and close her eyes. But that wasn't going to happen until she recovered her purse. What was she going to do? Go to the police station?

She sighed. She could call home, but it was her absolute last option. If her father heard about this accident, he'd be adamant that she return home immediately. She wasn't going to do that. Not until she figured out this secret because she felt as though it were very important. There had been this look in her mother's eyes when she'd attempted to tell her—was it desperation? Or maybe fear?

Lainey didn't even know if she was looking in the right direction. All she had to go on was some vague journal entries her mother had written and her gut instinct. *Wait. The journal!*

Her chest tightened when she realized the journal was in her luggage—luggage that at this point was missing. Could this day get any worse?

"Excuse me." A male voice drew her from her thoughts.

She turned and spotted Jack—the man with the mysterious dark eyes. He had broad shoulders and muscular biceps. She wondered what it would be like to be held in his strong embrace.

As quickly as the thought came to her, she felt the heat of embarrassment rush to her face and set her cheeks aflame. What was wrong with her? She never had these sorts of reactions upon meeting someone. It must be the bump on the head.

"Jack, right?" She didn't know why she'd said that, probably because it was the thought that came to mind. It was much better than saying: *you're the most handsome man I've ever met.* Definitely better than that.

He nodded. "Should you be up moving around?"

She shrugged. Big mistake. Her right shoulder sent a sharp arrow pain through her chest. She would have to remember to skip the shrugging until her bumps and bruises healed. "I'm not fond of hospitals, so the doc said if I came back for an exam tomorrow that he'd let me go home."

"Maybe you should stay here. You look..." The words died on his lips.

She could only imagine what she must look like by now. Deciding it was best to change the subject, she said, "I need to get a room for the night. I'd ask for a recommendation, but first I need to find my things."

"Your things?"

"Yeah. You know...my purse and my luggage." She didn't want to dump all of her problems onto him. "Are you here to see someone else?" When he shook his head, she asked, "You waited all of this time to see me?"

"I wanted to make sure you were okay. I feel really bad about what happened."

"I'm fine." When his eyes clouded with disbelief, she said, "Really. You don't have to worry about me."

She was touched he was so concerned, but she didn't need him worrying about her. The headache would eventually fade away. Not soon enough as far as she was concerned, but there was nothing Jack could do about that.

He must have had a front row seat for her accident—the one that she couldn't remember. She felt as though she were forgetting something else. Something important. It was on the fringe of her thoughts, but she couldn't retrieve it.

Chapter Five

He should walk away.

She wasn't his responsibility.

And yet Jack's feet refused to move.

He was lying to himself. He'd played a large part in her being at the medical center. And he felt awful about the accident.

He was a bit surprised she was being released so quickly. He would have thought they'd transfer her to the mainland or something. It appeared her injuries weren't as serious as he'd initially thought. The tension in his chest eased.

His gaze took in the redness and the beginning of a bruise along her temple. That had to hurt. He wished there was something he could do to help her feel better. "Where are you staying on the island?"

She blinked as she looked at him. She was quiet for a moment. "I don't know."

"Do you know anyone on the island?"

She gave a shake of her head before grimacing in pain. "No. I don't. But I'm sure I can get a hotel room."

So, she didn't feel as fine as she wanted him to believe. "Well, if you don't have any place picked out, I highly recommend the Brass Anchor Inn."

Just then Doc Mullins stepped into the room. Jack had known the doctor his whole life. In fact, Doc Mullins had delivered not only himself but all of his siblings. Now that the doc was retiring, Jack had no idea who would take over the man's position, because he was more than just a doctor; he was a true part of the community. He knew his patients by their first names and was truly interested in what was going on in their lives.

"Hey, Jack." Doc approached him. He withdrew a business card and pen from the pocket of his white coat. He wrote something on the back of the card before holding it out to him. "Here's my new cell number."

Jack accepted the card and glanced down at the number on the back. Why did Doc give him his private cell number?

Doc's gaze flickered to Lainey before returning to him. "Keep a close eye on her. If she has any symptoms such as throwing up, her headache worsens, or a change in her vision, call me. Basically if you are worried, call me. It doesn't matter what time it is." His gaze moved to Lainey. "I really wish you'd change your mind about being transferred to the mainland."

Wait. Doc Mullins thought he was caring for Lainey. How in the world had he gotten that idea?

"Hey, Doc." Jack had to clarify things. "I'm not sure..."

"Don't worry, Jack. I'll fill you in on everything." Lainey sent the doctor a smile that didn't quite reach her eyes. "There's nothing to worry about. I'm fine."

Doc frowned but didn't say another word as he moved on.

Jack had absolutely no idea what had just happened? Did Doc think Lainey was his girlfriend? If so, he knew exactly who had given him that impression. The question that nagged at him was: why?

Jack's curious gaze settled on the beautiful woman in front of him. "Do you know what he's talking about?"

Lainey glanced away. "I can explain."

He had a feeling he wasn't going to like what she had to say. "I'm listening."

She glanced around the waiting area, which was quickly filling with young and old alike. "Not here."

He followed her toward the exit.

"Excuse me." A woman behind the reception desk called out to her.

Lainey looked in the lady's direction. "Are you talking to me?"

The woman nodded.

Lainey made her way over to the window. "Yes?"

"I still need your medical insurance." The woman looked expectantly at her.

"Um..." Lainey had a deer-in-headlights look.

"She lost her purse in the accident," Jack said. "Can she bring it by as soon as her purse is located?"

The woman slipped a bill through the window. "This needs to be paid before you leave. If you don't have insurance, we take credit cards."

Lainey's face paled. "But I don't have a credit card either. It's with my insurance card. And I don't know where that is right now."

The woman frowned at Lainey. "How are you going to pay?"

Lainey reached into her pocket and pulled out some cash. Her gaze moved to the total on the bill and then she counted the cash. "It's not the whole amount, but it'll cover some of it."

Jack felt bad for her. It was bad enough that she'd been in an accident and had problems with her memory, but now she was struggling to pay for her medical care. And he couldn't escape his guilt at his part in all of this.

He reached into his pocket and pulled out his wallet. He withdrew his credit card and held it out to the woman. "Put the charge on here."

"Don't do that," Lainey said to the woman before she whirled around to him. "You can't do that."

The woman behind the window hesitated, her gaze moving between the two of them.

Jack nodded for the woman to go ahead and put the charge on his card. Then he turned his attention to Lainey. "It's fine. You can pay me back later."

"It's not fine." She glanced over to see the woman was already processing the charge. "How do you even know that I'll pay you back?"

He shrugged. "I have a good feeling about you."

"But you don't know me."

He pursed his lips as his gaze narrowed in on her. "Are you always this disagreeable with people that try to help you?"

She reached into her pocket and withdrew the wad of cash again. She held it out to him. "Here. Take this."

He didn't make any motion to take it. "You keep it. It's all the money you have until you remember where your things are."

Her fine brows drew together in a stubborn line. "Take it. Please."

"I can wait for you to pay me back." When she attempted to shove the money at him, he backed up. "Seriously. You're going to need it for food and stuff."

She expelled a resigned sigh, and he subdued a smile.

A few minutes later, they made their way outside. They hadn't even made it two steps beyond the doorway when he turned to her. The gusty wind swept a lock of her hair in her face. It took all of his willpower to resist the urge to reach out and tuck it behind her ear.

As she swiped aside her hair, he asked, "Why does the doctor think you're staying with me?"

"It's not a big deal. The doctor was making a fuss out of me staying in the hospital for the night, and I told him I wasn't going to do it. So, he insisted I stay with someone tonight. And you're the only one I know on the island."

"But you don't know me."

She smiled and shrugged. "I know. I was desperate. I just couldn't stay there. Don't worry about it. I'll just get a room at a hotel."

"First, there are no hotels on the island. There are some inns and B and Bs. Second, you have a head injury, so you need to stay with someone in case you have any problems."

Her eyes widened. "But I can't stay with you. I don't even know you."

He thought of a compromise. "No worries. You don't have to stay with me. Just give me a moment."

He held up a finger as he pulled his phone from his pocket. He dialed his mother. She answered on the first ring. "Hey, Mom, what are you doing?"

"Your father and I are visiting with your aunt and uncle." As she continued to talk, he recalled their trip to see his mother's family in Maine. "Why? What do you need?"

The stress of the day had him forgetting about his parents' trip. "Oh, nothing. I was just checking in. I forgot you were out of town."

They talked for a few more minutes. He didn't want to alert his mother that anything was wrong. He ended the call and slipped his phone back into his pocket.

Lainey arched a brow. "Were you planning to pawn me off on your mother?"

"Yes. But I forgot they are out of town for the week." He searched his thoughts for another alternative. "I could call my sister."

"Your sister?"

He nodded. "She owns the Brass Anchor Inn."

She smiled. "It seems like no matter where I choose to stay that I'm going to be staying with one of your relatives. Does your family own the entire island or something?"

He smiled back. "No. There's just a lot of us. I have five siblings and lots of extended family."

"Wow. There are a lot of you."

"So which shall it be, the inn or my place? I can sleep on the couch and let you have the bed."

"Are you always so generous to strangers?"

He shook his head. "Not always."

"So you're just making an exception for me?" Her gaze searched his. When he didn't respond, she said, "I don't want to impose on you. I'll stay at the inn."

He would be lying if he were to deny being disappointed at not having an unexpected house guest. But he couldn't blame her. He still wasn't sure how to keep an eye on her when she was at the inn. He'd have to give that some more thought because he didn't want anything else to happen to her.

Chapter Six

The sun was so bright.

Too bright.

Lainey blamed it on her worsening headache. She refused to consider that it was because her concussion was as severe as the doctor had alluded to. She would be fine. She had to be. She had a mission to accomplish—a secret to unravel—an answer to find.

She just wished she could remember what had brought her to Bluestar Island. She had to be following a lead. Right? That had to be it.

"My cart is over here." Jack's voice drew her from her thoughts. "Are you feeling all right?"

Her head hurt, but she didn't know if it was from the bump on her head or the fact that she couldn't recall her most recent memories—not since she arrived in Boston a few days ago. If only she could find her luggage with her mother's journal inside, maybe it would jar her memories.

She glanced over to find Jack was still staring at her with an expectant look. "I'm fine. Stop worrying."

He didn't say anything as they took a seat in his cart. For a moment, he reached out as though to place the key in the ignition but then hesitated.

She grew concerned. "Is everything all right?"

He blinked and shoved the key into the ignition. As the engine started, he said, "Sorry. I just remembered something."

"About me?"

He shook his head. "No. It's about my work. But I'll deal with it later."

"I'm sorry to interrupt your day." Guilt settled on her shoulders. He had really gone out of his way for her, from checking on her at the little hospital-like place to paying her hospital bill. She would pay him back. If she could just remember where she'd left her things. "If you could just give me directions, I can walk to the B and B."

"I don't think so. After all, you told the doc I'd keep an eye on you, and I intend to keep your word to him."

"But you don't have to—"

"I want to."

The man beside her was quite stubborn. She didn't understand why he was going out of his way for her. Surely, he had to get back to his work as well as a wife—her gaze strayed to his left hand, his finger was bare—or perhaps a girlfriend.

"Are you sure your girlfriend won't mind you helping me?" The words were out of her mouth before she realized she'd vocalized her thoughts. Heat started in her chest and worked its way up to her cheeks. She didn't know a way to walk back the words, so she said nothing.

"I don't have a girlfriend." His words were clipped.

She had a feeling there was more to that statement than what he was willing to admit. She wanted to ask him another question about his social life, but this time she refrained.

She couldn't deny the fact he was single was welcome news. Not that she was interested in dating him or anything. She had her hands full with trying to fill in the gaps in her memory and locating her possessions. Still, it was nice to know she wasn't stepping on any toes by accepting his help.

As they slowly drove across the island, the setting sun sent a warm glow over the town. She focused on taking in some of Bluestar. The small town was picturesque. She loved how colorful the shops were, from a pastel yellow-and-white-striped awning to a pink-painted storefront.

She reached for her camera to photograph the images. Only the camera—her mother's old camera—wasn't hanging around her neck. "Do you know what happened to my camera?"

Jack shook his head. "I never saw it."

Did she have it with her at the time of the accident? Once again, she couldn't remember. She hoped not. The camera was a fond memory of her mother—something they had in common.

"Do you remember when you last saw it?" When she shook her head, he said, "Maybe you lost it during the accident." He slammed the brakes and made a sharp left.

"Where are we going?"

"Back to the scene of the accident." He let off the accelerator and glanced at her. "Is that all right with you?"

Since she still couldn't remember anything about the accident, it wasn't going to bother her. "It's fine by me. Do you think my things are still there?"

"It's hard to tell. The sheriff might have grabbed your bag if he noticed it. I'll give him a call."

While Jack spoke on the phone, she wondered if it would be possible to get a new phone on the island. They had a lot of quaint shops, but she hadn't seen any that looked like they were selling cell phones, but she refused to give up hope.

They turned a corner and headed down a busy street. She spotted something that looked like a lighthouse. What was it doing in the middle of the town? Wasn't a lighthouse supposed to be along the coastline?

When Jack parked, she was able to see the sign attached to the lighthouse. It said that it was a café. So, it wasn't a real lighthouse but rather a replica. *Interesting*.

She got out and joined Jack on the side of the road. She did a quick scan and didn't see anything. Her hopes were dashed.

Jack walked around the area. She didn't think he was going to find anything. If her possessions had been here, they were gone now.

After they'd spoken to some of the surrounding businesses to see if anyone had turned in her purse or suitcase, they weren't any closer to finding them than they'd been before. On the way back to the cart, Jack was still looking around.

He kicked at some old dried-up leaves that had gathered in the ditch. "Hey, what's this?"

She rushed over to find him moving aside some debris. He pulled on something and then lifted a...camera. Her camera. Her mother's camera.

"That's it. That's my camera."

His brows drew together as he examined it.

"What's wrong?" She reached for it.

When she took it in her hand, she realized what his worried look was for. The lens was shattered, and a large crack ran the length of the camera as though it had been run over. A sadness fell over her. It was ruined. Tears burned the backs of her eyes. She blinked them away. It felt like she'd just lost another tie to her mother.

"I'm really sorry." Jack's voice was soft and full of sympathy.

"It's not your fault. It was an accident." With the camera in hand, she moved back to the cart. "Let's go to the inn."

She held the broken camera as they rode through town. She knew it was pointless to keep it, but she wasn't ready to part with it yet.

When the beach came into sight, she was impressed. The large beach was clean and welcoming. If her head didn't hurt, she would have elected to go for a stroll along the water's edge. Maybe she would do that later.

The ocean became obscured by green foliage and houses. She wondered if her mother had ever been on this charming island. If so, Lainey was surprised her mother ever wanted to leave.

"We're here." Jack pulled the cart to a stop in a parking spot.

Lainey gazed up at the large blue Victorian-looking building. The sign in the front yard said it was the Brass Anchor Inn. Charming was the first word that came to mind.

They stepped out of the cart and made their way up the sidewalk. While Jack rushed up the two steps and moved swiftly to the white French doors, she took her time. She took in the wide porch that was lined with white rocking chairs. There were small tables between them for drinks and a potted plant. Once again, the word charming came to mind.

"Hey." Jack held the open door for her. "Are you coming?"

She hurried her steps. Once they were inside the spacious lobby, it took a moment for her eyes to adjust after being out in the bright sunshine. She took in the gray wood tile floors with a royal blue runner that led from the door to the check-in desk. Her gaze meandered around the room, admiring the comfortable-looking furnishings that portrayed a sense of coziness.

She paused and glanced off to the side, taking in the display cases with lots of seafaring memorabilia. On the walls was a collection of framed photographs. She wanted to meander over to check it all out, but Jack was already at the check-in desk, waiting for her.

She moved to his side. There was no one working the desk. Noticing a brass Victorian style bell, she tapped her fingers on it. *Ding.*

"Coming," a male voice called out from the office behind the desk. A moment later, an older man stepped out of the office. "Sorry to keep you waiting."

The man wore a dark blue polo shirt with the inn's logo embroidered with white thread and a gold pin with the name Harvey Coleman. His snow-white hair was kept short. He had a close-trimmed mustache and beard. Immediately the thought of Santa Claus came to mind.

When the man's gaze settled on Jack, he said, "Hey Jack. What can I do for you?"

"We need a room," Jack said.

Lainey couldn't believe he'd just said that. She lightly elbowed him aside. "What he meant to say is I need a room."

Jack frowned at her but remained quiet.

Harvey's gaze moved between the two of them. A smile played at the corners of his mouth. "It doesn't matter which of you needs the room. We don't have any available."

"What?" Jack's dark brows drew together. "Are you sure?"

"I'm absolutely positive." Harvey's tone was firm.

And then she had an idea. She struggled not to get her hopes up, but if she was right about this, it would make her life so much easier. "Could you tell me if Lainey Dell is registered here?"

The breath hitched in her lungs as Harvey glanced down at the computer and ran his fingers over the keyboard. *Please let my name be in their system. Please let my belongings be here.*

The moment seemed to go on forever. Harvey frowned at the computer before he typed something else.

When he lifted his gaze to meet hers, he said, "I'm sorry, but there's no one registered with that name."

"That's okay," Lainey said. "Maybe I can get a room at one of the other B and Bs on the island."

Harvey's expression wasn't hopeful. "It's doubtful you'll find any vacancies."

Jack leaned against the counter. "What's going on?"

"There's a big wedding on the island this weekend. But come Sunday, we'll have plenty of rooms."

"That won't help us right now," Jack said.

"I'm really sorry," Harvey said. "I'd help you if I could."

They thanked him for his help, and then they left. Lainey squinted as soon as they walked back out into the bright sunlight. She was going to have to buy herself some sunglasses because her head hurt, and the brightness was only making it worse.

She joined Jack in the cart. She didn't know what to say. If the pounding in her head would just let up, she'd be able to form a plan.

"You don't look so good," Jack said.

"Gee, thanks. You certainly know how to flatter a girl."

Under other circumstances, she would just take the ferry back to the mainland where there would be plenty of available hotel rooms. But she couldn't leave this island until she remembered what had happened to her belongings—most especially her mother's journal.

So far nothing had come back to her. The last couple of days were a total blank. The doctor said the memories may or may not come back to her. He told her to be grateful she knew who she was and where she came from.

Chapter Seven

He'd missed his very **important meeting.**

Now his phone was blowing up with messages.

It was late into the evening as Jack and Lainey climbed into his cart. They were going to head to the Brass Anchor Inn. Jack took a moment to scroll through his messages, only pausing when he saw one from his boss. They had pushed back his presentation, but there was no specific date assigned for the rescheduled meeting. It was a we'll-get-to-it-eventually feel to the email. He wanted something more specific. He needed to fix this. But there was nothing he could do about it right now.

"Is everything all right?" she asked.

He turned the phone off and looked at her. "What?"

"You were frowning, and then you sighed. Listen, if I'm taking up too much of your time, we can go our separate ways."

"No." He pushed his worries to the back of his mind. "It had nothing to do with you."

"I take it something is the matter. Can I help?"

He shook his head. "It was just an update on a project I've been working on, but I don't want to talk about it. I'd rather hear what you think about your visit to Bluestar."

"I don't know." When he gave her a puzzled look, she said, "What I mean is my short-term memory is spotty, and I can't remember anything about the island. The doctor said my memory lapse might clear up with a little time, or those pieces of my memory might be gone for good. At least I know who I am, so there's that. I just can't help but feel as though I've forgotten something very important. And for the life of me I can't figure out what it is."

He started the motor. "Maybe some rest will help."

As they passed by a couple of carts, Lainey asked, "Why don't they allow cars on the island?"

"I'm not sure. It was decided long before my time. But I like it, except for in the winter."

"What happens in the winter?"

"We have covers for the carts and use portable heaters that plug in, but it's not as warm as a car with heated seats. Luckily, the town is small, so there isn't a lot of traveling."

"Interesting. What else is unique about this island?"

He shrugged as he slowed as he approached an intersection with a stop sign. "I don't know. For me, it isn't unique."

"So, you were born here?"

He nodded. "I've lived here all of my life." As though to prove him right, the Murrays smiled and waved at him. He waved back. "But I'm planning on moving in the near future."

Now why had he said that? He hadn't even told his family about his plans yet. He knew his siblings would understand, but his mother would beg him to stay. And he couldn't do that. He was constantly reminded of the life he didn't have—the one that had crashed and died.

He pushed the painful thoughts to the back of his mind. He knew they wouldn't stay there long. Come the night, they would creep into his thoughts and sometimes his nightmares.

Lainey's voice drew his attention. "Where are you moving to?"

He welcomed the distraction. "New York City."

"Wow. That's a big move. Why do you want to trade in this cozy island for big city life?"

He shrugged. "It's for work."

That wasn't a lie. It just wasn't the main reason he wanted to get away from the island. Every time he turned around, his siblings were falling in love. He was happy for them, but they were a reminder of the life he'd once had.

To make matters worse, people were always trying to set him up. It wasn't just his family. Friends were certain they knew the perfect woman for him. The truth was he didn't want to date. He didn't deserve to be happy like that again—not after the accident and subsequent divorce.

Before Lainey could ask him any other questions, he said, "You still have the option of staying at my place."

He could feel her surprised gaze on him as she said, "I couldn't do that."

"Yes, you can. And then I'd be able to keep my word to Doc and make sure you're all right tonight. How are you feeling?"

"I'm fine."

He knew that was just a pat answer. "Don't tell me what you think I want to hear. How do you really feel?"

She was quiet for a moment, as though considering her answer. "I'm tired and my head still hurts."

He turned the cart in the direction of his apartment. "Then you can lie down for a bit and see if it helps."

"You mean at your place?" There was hesitation in her voice.

"Yes. I'm a good guy." Was he? Maybe he should amend that. "You can trust me. And if you don't believe me..." He pulled the cart over to the side of the road and stopped. Along came Ethan Walker, local fire chief. "Hey, Ethan, am I trustworthy?"

Ethan's brows drew together as he stopped next to the cart. "What's going on?"

"Just answer the question, am I trustworthy?"

Ethan's confused gaze moved between Jack and Lainey. "Of course you are. Why?"

"Thanks. I'll see you at the party tomorrow night." Jack pressed the accelerator.

Lainey let out a laugh. "I can't believe you just did that."

"Would you like to pick someone out to ask?" He pointed to Molly Simpson, a waitress at the Lighthouse Café. "How about her?" He pointed to Sam Bell, a local farmer. "Or what about him?"

When he slowed down, she said, "Don't stop. I believe you."

"Are you sure?"

She smiled. "Yes. But I have one question."

"What's that?"

"How far is it to your place?" A yawn escaped her berry red lips.

"Not far." He smiled at her. "And while you rest, I'll order us some dinner. How does pizza sound?"

"Good. Thank you for everything."

He didn't know why he was smiling. He was just helping out someone in need. That was all. It wasn't like he was interested in her or anything.

Her eyes fluttered open.

Lainey yawned and stretched. Her body protested the movement. Her left shoulder was sore. Her head still ached though it wasn't as intense as it had been right after the accident.

She froze as she glanced around the unfamiliar bedroom. Her heart lodged in her throat. Where was she?

It took her a moment to remember she was in Jack's bedroom. She exhaled a suspended breath.

As the reality of her current situation came back to her, she hoped it meant that all her memories had returned. She searched her thoughts. Try as she might, the holes in her memory still remained.

She'd only meant to fall asleep for a little bit, but as she looked at the window, the sun was rising in the sky. She glanced at the bedside clock. It was past eight o'clock. That meant she'd slept for almost twelve hours. She had been a lot more tired than she'd thought.

Her gaze moved around the bedroom, finding it neat and orderly. There was a tall chest of drawers, but there weren't any framed photos on it nor were there any on the bedside tables. In fact, there was nothing on top of the chest. He apparently didn't believe in decorations.

She got out of bed and made the bed—Jack's bed. It wasn't hard with just a dark gray sheet and a red comforter to straighten. She couldn't believe he'd let her sleep that long. Then again, he was probably relieved he didn't have to deal with her. He'd already gone out of his way for her. No one had ever been so generous toward her with their time or money.

If her circumstances were different, she would have liked to get to know Jack better. As soon as the thought came to her, she pushed it away. That wasn't the point of her trip. The real problem was that she couldn't recall the exact reason for her trip to the island. She had the feeling it had something to do with her mother's secret, but it was only a guess.

She made her way out of the bedroom. Her head had hurt so much, and she'd been so tired when they'd arrived that she hadn't taken time to take in her surroundings. Jack kept his place neat and tidy. It was the opposite of her. She was always in such a rush that she just didn't have time to put things where they belonged.

As an attorney at her father's business, she was always called in on one meeting after the other. Of course, that was just an excuse she told herself because she was never a neat freak, not even close to it, not even when she was young.

When her mother had stated she couldn't even walk in Lainey's room because of all the toys, Lainey had gotten down on her hands and knees. She'd crawl through her room swiping toys to the left and right, creating a path to her bed and another to the closet. Her mother had not been impressed with her ingenuity.

"You're awake."

She glanced around to find Jack sitting at a desk in the corner of the living room. He appeared to have been working at a computer. He shut it down before she was able to see what was on the large screen.

"I am. Thank you for the use of your room."

"No problem." His voice held a friendly tone.

He swiveled his desk chair to face her. "I wanted to let you know that I called around to the other B and Bs on the island, and I'm sorry to say that they don't have you registered as a guest, and they don't have any vacancies."

"Thank you. I really appreciate it."

She still felt bad that he was going out of his way for her. Her gaze moved to the black screen and then back to him. Their gazes caught and held. Her heart sped up. How had she missed how his dark eyes seemed to be bottomless? She felt if she stared into them long enough, she would drown in them. She stared perhaps a moment too long but just long enough for heat to rush to her cheeks.

She glanced away and swallowed hard. "Did I interrupt you?"

He glanced over his shoulder at the blank monitor before turning back to her. "I just catching up on some emails. How are you feeling?"

"I'm okay."

"Can I get you something to eat?"

She'd fallen asleep before eating dinner. Her stomach rumbled in protest. "That would be nice. But you don't have to wait on me. I can cook."

"You can rest and I'll get it." When he smiled, her stomach dipped.

When he once again caught her staring at him for a moment too long, the heat returned to her face. She glanced away. "After that I should get out of your way."

"Not so fast." He moved to the refrigerator and pulled out a dozen eggs. "The doctor said you needed someone to stay with you for twenty-four hours."

She struggled not to roll her eyes. "I'm not a child."

He straightened from where he was peering into the fridge and turned to her. He arched a brow. "But you were in an accident, and you hit your head. So, you can stay here until the doctor releases you."

"Has anyone ever accused you of being stubborn?"

When he smiled, twin dimples showed in his cheeks. Her stomach did that somersault thing again. She wondered if anyone had ever told him how cute he was. She imagined that plenty of women had alerted him to this fact.

He arched a brow. "I could say the same thing about you."

She moved toward the kitchen. "Do you mind if I get something to drink?"

"I'll get it for you." He opened a cabinet and withdrew a glass. "What would you like?" He turned back to the fridge, as though to see what he had to offer her. "I don't have much."

"Water is fine."

While he filled the glass with tap water, she took a seat at the counter. When he placed it in front of her, she said, "Thank you. But you don't have to wait on me."

"Mrr…"

Lainey's head jerked around, searching for the source of the sound. Her gaze settled on a big black cat with a white chest and white feet that made it look like he was wearing booties. The cat stood on the edge of the rug, yawning before he stretched. It looked like she wasn't the only one to have woken up from a nap.

Lainey turned back to Jack. "You didn't tell me that you had a roommate."

"Oh. Sorry. I forgot to introduce you to Tux."

"Is he friendly?" When Jack nodded, she immediately approached the cat. She knelt down, and Tux immediately sniffed her hands. When Tux rubbed over her, she reached out and pet his back. Tux's fur was thick and velvety. It shined in the rays of the late-afternoon sun. "Can I pick him up?"

"I'm sure he won't mind. He loves attention."

That was all the invitation she needed. She scooped up the cat and straightened. Tux didn't seem to mind as he purred and rubbed his head along her chin. A smile pulled at Lainey's lips. She'd never had a pet of her own, but it didn't mean she didn't love animals.

"He definitely likes you." Jack leaned back against the kitchen counter.

She continued to cuddle Tux. There was just something about petting the cat and feeling the vibration of his purr that relaxed her. Maybe when she got back to New York, she would consider adopting a cat.

In no time at all, Jack served them up some fried eggs and toast. She was impressed with his perfect over-easy eggs. She was so hungry that she had three slices of toast. Even with all of the food, her headache persisted. Jack gave her two pain killers.

After their leisurely breakfast, she insisted on cleaning up. With her head still bothering her, Jack suggested that she lay down again. She really didn't want to. There was so much she wanted to do, like find her belongings. She just needed this headache to subside.

And so she did as he suggested and returned to the bedroom. The truth was that she hadn't been sleeping well lately—at least the parts that she could remember. She laid her head on the pillow, telling herself she'd get back up as soon as the pain killers kicked in. There was no way she could sleep any longer but the pillow soft and the bed was cozy. She felt herself relaxing and soon she dozed off for a little bit.

When she returned to the living room, she found Jack once again sitting at his computer. She quietly made her way to the kitchen for some water.

"I'm almost done," Jack said as his fingers moved rapidly over the keyboard. "There." He turned to her. "How are you feeling?"

"I'm okay."

"I think we should head over to the medical center and let the doctor check you out." He got up from his desk chair. "And afterward, what would you like to do?"

Her immediate answer was to go find her stuff, but without her memory, she had no idea where to even begin to hunt for her things. Her gut told her that her things were on the island but where?

Not wanting to disrupt his life any further than she already had, she asked, "What would you be doing if I wasn't here?"

He rubbed the back of his neck. "I'd be getting ready to go to a surprise party."

"That sounds nice."

He shook his head. "Oh, no. It isn't going to be nice at all."

Her eyes widened. "Don't you like the person?"

"It's not that. Actually, the guy used to be the town scrooge, but that all changed this past Christmas."

"So, you're throwing a party for this guy?"

He shook his head again. "I'm not throwing the party. It was my brother's girlfriend's idea. I'm only bringing some cookies. In fact, Melinda, my brother's girlfriend, is the one that brought about the change in Blackwell." When Lainey sent him a puzzled look, he said, "The party is for a guy named Horace Blackwell."

"If the guy changed from being a scrooge to someone that people want to throw a party in his honor, I don't think you should miss it. Especially not for my sake. I can just stay here with Tux." She hugged the cat before she bent over and placed him gently on the floor.

"You don't understand. My hesitancy about going has nothing to do with Blackwell."

"Now you have me curious. Why don't you want to go?" He was quiet for a moment, as though he were hesitant to tell her. And then realizing she'd been too forward, a side effect of her job as an attorney, she said, "Just forget I asked."

"No. It's okay. It's just that there are a bunch of well-meaning people in this town, and they're insistent on playing matchmaker. In fact, one of the ladies is planning to set me up with her niece tonight at the party."

"And you don't care for her niece?"

"I've never met her niece. But no, I don't want to be set up on a blind date or any other kind of date. It's just another reason why I want to move to New York."

She felt bad for him. She remembered how her well-meaning friends used to try to fix her up with friends and friends of friends. She'd never had one of those dates go beyond the initial meeting. "Would you go to the party if it wasn't for the matchmaking?"

He shrugged. "Probably."

"Then why don't you go tonight, and I'll be your date." When his eyes suddenly widened, she knew she'd said it all wrong. "What I mean is I'll be your fake date. If you want."

His brows scrunched together. "Why would you want to do that?"

"Why not? You've gone out of your way for me. It's the least I can do."

"Are you sure you feel up to it?"

She nodded. "When do we leave?" She glanced down at her clothes. "Then again. I don't have anything else to wear."

"The party is at seven at the bookshop."

"The bookshop. Now I really am intrigued."

"As for your clothes, the party is casual so you're dressed fine. But we could leave early, and you could pick out some new clothes, if you like. You know, for tomorrow. Just until you get your belongings back."

She retrieved her phone from her pocket and stared at the smashed screen. "And can we stop somewhere so I can get my phone replaced?"

He paused. "Yeah. Sure. We should probably get going. I don't know how long we'll have to wait at the medical center. Afterward we can go to the Lighthouse Café and grab something to eat. Do you like burgers and fries?"

She nodded as her stomach rumbled its approval. "Sounds good."

After she recalled the cash in her pocket, she felt better about agreeing to dinner. The only problem was the cash wouldn't last her long. There had to be some way for her to get her hands on more money without alerting her father to her location and the fact that she'd lost her purse. She would have to give it some more thought.

Chapter Eight

WHAT HAD SHE BEEN thinking?

Lainey honestly didn't want to spend the evening on a fake date. Her headache came rushing back, and the pain killers only took the edge off the pain. So, the thought of walking through Bluestar with Jack wasn't high on her list of things to do.

She'd much rather curl up on his couch with Tux and watch television. But she figured Jack had gone so far out of his way for her that she owed it to him to be his plus one. This way he could enjoy the evening without having an unwanted date forced upon him.

The visit to the medical center took much longer than she'd been expecting. The doctor once again urged her to go to the mainland hospital for more thorough tests, but she insisted her head didn't hurt as much as it had the day before. The doctor instructed she come back the next day and she agreed.

Next on their agenda was a visit to The Lighthouse Café. It was the cutest restaurant she'd ever seen. It was built like a scaled-down model of a lighthouse. To her utter surprise, after a late lunch or an early dinner, depending on how you looked at it, her headache mostly subsided. Maybe she had just been hungry. She hoped that was the case.

Sadly, the store that sold cell phones was closed. She would make sure to return first thing in the morning. Being without her phone was so unnerving. She felt so disconnected from the world. Or maybe it was her spotty memory that was making her feel that way.

Afterward, she did some bargain shopping and picked up some new outfits. When Jack offered to pay...again, she'd refused and spent some of the cash in her pocket. It was a good thing her mother had taught her to keep enough cash on hand just in case of an emergency. Although, she suspected her mother never imagined this sort of emergency.

Before they went to the party, Jack insisted they had to stop by The Elegant Bakery. A bell above the door jingled as they entered. Lainey stopped just inside the doorway in order to take it all in. The bakery had white walls with black trim and brass fixtures.

Wow! The place certainly lived up to its name. It was no wonder it appeared to attract so many customers.

Lainey inhaled. She detected scents of cinnamon, butter, and so much more. If the baked goods tasted half as delicious as they smelled, she knew why all of these people were in line.

As they took a spot at the end of the line, she took in the large room. In the middle was a round pedestal table. The light-colored wood was whitewashed. There was a certain classic elegance to it.

In the center of the table was a white lace doily with a black three-tier cupcake stand. The colorful cupcakes on the shelves were the real show-stoppers. Whipped frosting in pastel pink, green, blue, and yellow was adorned with coarse sugar that glittered beneath the lighting. They were almost too pretty to eat.

She lifted her chin and stared up at a crystal and brass chandelier. The six-candle structure with all the crystal dangling from it twinkled like diamonds. This was by far the most beautiful bakery she'd ever been in.

As they moved to the front of the line, she noticed a giant gold-framed chalkboard behind the counter. On the left side was written in white chalk: *Welcome to the Elegant Bakery*. On the right side was a list of items and prices.

Her gaze lowered to the row of display cases that lined the back wall of the bakery. Bright lights in the cases highlighted all of the delicious temptations.

She wanted to sample some of everything. After her delicious dinner at the Lighthouse Café, this was definitely a case of her eyes being bigger than her stomach, but how was one to choose just one decadent treat when they all looked so delicious?

"This place is amazing," she honestly said.

Jack sent her a knowing smile. "It's why I don't visit it very often. It's impossible to leave with just one or two items."

She gazed off to the side. Was that a whoopie pie? She hadn't had one of those since she was a kid. A couple of times a year, her mother would take her on road trips to the Pennsylvania Dutch area where they baked the most delicious whoopie pies with fluffy white frosting in the center. The memory edged out some of the sadness in order to make room in her heart for some happiness.

"Did you see something you want?" Jack's voice drew her from her thoughts.

"Uh." It wasn't like she needed a whoopie pie. She turned away. "It's nothing."

"It's definitely something. I saw the way your eyes lit up. What is it that caught your attention? One of the cookies?"

She shook her head.

"I know. A cupcake."

She felt silly for getting excited over it, but she could tell by the intent look Jack was giving her that he wasn't going to give up until she told him. "It's the red velvet whoopie pie."

"Good. We'll get one of them."

She shook her head. "It's okay."

"I don't think you understand. I am definitely getting you one."

She felt like she needed to explain her excitement over the whoopie pies. "My mother used to buy them for me when I was a kid. Just the sight of them brings back a lot of memories."

"Good ones, I hope."

"Definitely." She smiled and nodded. "I know I have a lot of holes in my recent memories, but the memories from my distant past are still intact." She told him about the trips her and her mother took from New York City to Lancaster, Pennsylvania. It was a time for them to get away from the social circles that her father's business successes had thrust them into.

"Do you and your mother still take road trips?"

Lainey could feel the smile slip from her face. "No. We don't."

As though he could sense the change in her mood, Jack started telling her about the bakery, which was under new management and had been recently remodeled.

She enjoyed listening to him talk, and she was surprised by how easy it was to open up to him. There was something special about Jack. And apparently she wasn't the only one to think so as she'd noticed the great number of Bluestar residents that had taken time to speak to him that day. If only she was going to stay on the island longer, she could imagine them forming a close friendship.

Two red velvet whoopie pies.

Jack couldn't resist ordering them while Lainey was meandering around the bakery. It was the first time since the accident that he'd seen her light up. He longed to see that look on her face again.

The whoopie pies could be her late-night snack and her breakfast, if she wanted. He might even go back to the bakery in the morning to get her more. He enjoyed making her smile.

As they made their way to the Seaside Bookshop, he answered Lainey's questions about the town and the many small businesses. He'd never met someone who asked so many questions about the island. Maybe she was hoping that something in the information he relayed to her would unlock her missing memories. If so, he was more than happy to assist her.

"Are you sure you don't want one of those whoopie pies now?" He dangled the white bag in front of her for the third time.

"You're being mean." She sent him a teasing smile. "You know I'm stuffed from our late lunch."

"Ah... So, you're admitting that you are tempted."

"Of course I am."

"Okay, but if you change your mind." He held up the bag again. "Just remember that I have the goods."

She lightly elbowed him as she rolled her eyes. "You are terrible."

Her smile broadened, puffing up her cheeks and making her eyes glitter like gems. She was really beautiful. The acknowledgment briefly stole his breath away.

Finding himself staring at her a moment too long, he glanced away. He couldn't let her get past his defenses. He had a plan not to get involved with anyone and move to the Big Apple. He was sticking to his plan.

Thankfully, the bookshop came into sight. He pointed at an older two-story brick building that had been whitewashed. "And there's our destination."

"I can't remember the last time I was in a bookshop. I used to love them when I was a kid. These days I just buy books on my phone, but it's just not the same." She glanced over at him. "Do you read?"

He nodded. "Sometimes. Not as much as my younger brother, Owen."

"What do you like to read?"

"Biographies and historical events. What about you?"

"Romance. I like the small-town ones. Maybe it's because I've always lived in a big city and wondered what it was like to live in one of the small towns that my mother and I would visit on our road trips."

They didn't have time to talk more because they'd arrived at the bookshop at precisely 6:45 p.m. as instructed by owner Melinda Coleman. They paused in front of the large showroom window, where there was a display that consisted of potted paper flowers in shades of pink, blue, red, purple, and yellow. Sitting in each of the large red clay flower pots was a book. Hanging down from the ceiling was a big yellow sun with a face that smiled at them.

Spring had most definitely sprung in Bluestar. In fact, Spring Fling was coming up in a couple of weeks. It was a big event for the residents. He wasn't planning to go, but if Lainey was still on the island, he might make an exception for her.

"I love this," Lainey said. "Do they always have such fun window displays?"

"Yes. Melinda, who owns the bookshop, is always creating unique and fun displays."

"I like her already."

"She's easy to like. She's one of the friendliest people in town. Just ask my brother Liam. They are always together."

"Are they married?"

"Not yet. But I expect they will be soon."

He let her climb the steps first and then followed. At the top, he pulled open the wooden door with a large glass window. Inside, the brass bell above the door jingled.

Most of the lights were turned off except for the ones over the checkout counter. He was surprised by the number of people who had shown up for the party. Melinda stood at the end of the checkout counter, surrounded by friends. When her gaze connected with his, her face lit up, and she waved.

They made his way through the crowd to where Melinda and Liam stood. "Nice turnout."

Melinda smile broadened. "I'm so happy this many people showed up."

"I'd like to introduce you to Lainey Dell." He turned to Lainey, watching to see if there was any recognition on her face of having met them previously. "Lainey, this is Melinda, who owns this wonderful bookshop, and my brother, Liam."

Lainey said hello to them and they asked how she was feeling after the accident. They mentioned that Lainey had been about to take their photo when the accident occurred. Jack hoped her memory would click in. There was no sparkle of recollection in her big brown eyes. That was too bad. Maybe she just needed some more time to get her memories back.

"I love your bookshop," Lainey said.

"Thank you," Melinda said. "Do you read much?"

Lainey nodded. They talked a little about books before Lainey glanced around. "There are a lot of people here."

She was right. The crowd kept growing. There were young and old alike. He'd guess there were at least a couple of dozen people, if not more. It was nice to see people giving Blackwell another chance. Kind of like Lainey was willing to give him a chance after their horrible first meet.

As Melinda and Liam turned to welcome some other guests, Lainey moved through the crowd to the side where there were rows of bookshelves. He meandered behind her.

She came to a stop near the front of the bookshop. "There are a lot of books here."

He couldn't help but smile. "It is a bookshop."

She gently elbowed him. "I know that. It's just this shop isn't that big, and yet they took advantage of every possible place to display books. Look." She pointed to one of the windows. "They even built bookshelves all around the window. Not a wasted space."

"You should tell Melinda how much you like the bookshop. She's been working really hard to fix it up. In fact, they just finished remodeling the other side of the shop."

Lainey followed him as they slowly worked their way back through the crowd to the other side of the bookshop. Every few steps, they would stop in order for Jack to greet people and introduce Lainey. Everyone was very friendly with Lainey. He could see how it put her at ease. And when the townsfolk asked how she was doing after the accident, she assured everyone that she was doing well.

When they reached the other side of the bookshop, he paused to take it in. This was the first time he'd seen the completed reading nook as Melinda fondly referred to the area. Without the bookshelves on this side, it was so much easier to move around. This section had been set up as a sitting area—a place where customers could take their purchases to read. And with the addition of the giant display window, it would provide them with a lot of natural light to read.

On the far wall was a long table covered with a white tablecloth and colorful balloons. The tabletop was filled with a variety of desserts from pie to cupcakes. They made their way over to the table and rearranged a few confectionary delights to make room for Jack's box of chocolate chip cookies.

His gaze moved over the table, taking in all of the delicious treats. "Want something?"

When he reached for a small piece of fudge, she reached for his hand. Her touch was gentle, but it felt as though static electricity arced between them. The charge raced up his arm and settled in his chest, making his heart thump harder.

Her gaze lifted to meet his. In that moment, he had the strongest urge to lean down and press his lips to hers. Just the thought had his pulse racing. What would she do if he acted on his impulse?

Would she shove him away? Probably. Or, would she kiss him back? The thought only made the urge that much stronger. His muscles tensed as it took every effort for him to resist the temptation because he imagined her kiss would be the sweetest treat of all.

Lainey jerked her hand away as though she'd felt the electrical current too. "Um... You have to wait until the birthday person gets their cake first."

He swallowed hard and hoped when he spoke that he sounded normal. "Is that some sort of rule?"

She rolled her eyes at him.

"It's a legit question," he insisted.

"Hey, Jack."

He turned around and found his brother Kent holding hands with his girlfriend, Sara Chen. "Hey, guys." Introductions and inquiries about Lainey's health were made before Jack said, "I see Josie over there with Lane. It looks like Melinda roped us all into attending."

"Not quite all of us. I haven't seen Owen," Kent said.

"Melinda probably didn't get a chance to invite him, since he's working round the clock to finish writing that video game," Jack said. "And of course, Grant is rarely around these days."

Kent shrugged. "Owen does get caught up in his work and hide away from the world."

Jack figured some day when the right woman came along that his little brother wouldn't get quite so wrapped up in his computer programming stuff.

"Too bad our little brother is so busy," Kent said. "I could really use his help at the store."

"Maybe you just need to hire some temporary help," Jack suggested.

Kent's brows rose. "What about you? You did okay helping me out yesterday."

Jack immediately shook his head. "I already have a full-time job." But then he got the beginning of an idea. "What kind of help are you looking for?"

"Someone to work the showroom floor and help people find what they are looking for."

"So, no heavy lifting?"

Kent shook his head. "Why? Do you have someone in mind?"

"As a matter of fact, I do." Jack's gaze moved to Lainey. "How would you feel about working at my family's furniture store?"

Her mouth opened, but no words came out. Apparently he'd caught her off guard. Maybe he should have run it past her in private, but he didn't want the opportunity to slip by her.

Lainey sent him a hesitant look. She was going to shoot down his idea without considering it. He knew this would be good for her. He didn't mind helping her out, but he also knew that she wasn't good with handouts.

To his surprise, Lainey spoke up. "I might be able to help."

Kent studied her. "Are you sure you feel up to it after the accident?"

She nodded. "I'm good. How long would you need help for?"

Kent looked as though he were giving the question some serious thought. "I'd say a week at most. I have a couple of people out on medical leave and another on vacation. But my parents will be back next week and will be able to fill in where necessary." Kent turned to Lainey. "I'm sorry my brother is putting you on the spot. I totally understand if you aren't interested in the position."

Lainey worried her bottom lip. "I'm not sure how much help I would be."

Kent smiled. "If that's your only hesitation, don't worry. I'll be there to answer any of your questions." He went on to tell her some of the particulars of the position.

Jack hoped she would take his brother up on the offer. It was only a temporary solution, but it would help her get back on her feet until she figured things out. Plus, he had to admit that he also had a selfish motive. If she took the job, she would remain on the island for a bit longer. It wasn't like he was planning to get serious with her. This was just a pleasant springtime distraction for the both of them.

A job?

Lainey was not expecting to receive a job offer this evening. She didn't anticipate being on the island for an entire week. She hadn't stayed in any location that long during her entire journey.

But there was something different about Bluestar. She felt like she fit in here. Perhaps it was the relaxed atmosphere—like attending a birthday party and not having to put on her finest dress for it.

Staying on the island would give her a chance to regain her memories. Maybe then she would finally know what had initially drawn her to this little island. And to find her belongings, including her mother's journal.

She really couldn't find any reason not to stay for the week. Her gaze met Kent's. "If you're sure I'll be a help and not a hindrance, then I'll take the job. Thank you for the offer."

"That's great." Sara's face lit up with a big smile. "We can get to know each other. Sometimes I bring Kent lunch. I'll bring extra on Monday so you can join us."

"I'd like that."

Melinda and Liam joined their group. Melinda practically beamed as she smiled at everyone. She looked like she was ready to burst with some sort of news. Lainey wanted to inquire but seeing as though they'd just met, she didn't feel it was her place. Instead, she stood there quietly as she waited to see if they'd share their news.

"I'm so glad you all made it to the party." Melinda's smile broadened.

"We're happy to be here," Sara said, "but I know that's not what has both of you grinning. So out with it. What's going on?"

Melinda glanced over at Liam. It was as though they were wordlessly communicating. And then they both turned to them.

Melinda pulled something out of her pocket. She slipped it on her finger and then held out her hand for everyone to see the sparkling diamond ring.

"Liam asked me to marry him. And I said yes." She let out a little squeal of excitement.

Everyone spoke at once, offering their congratulations. There were hugs and handshakes. There were questions about the upcoming wedding, for which both Melinda and Liam said they didn't have a date picked. And then someone asked how Liam's little boy felt about it, and Liam assured everyone that Tate was excited. He loved Melinda almost as much as his daddy did.

And then Melinda checked the time. "It's party time."

She moved behind the checkout counter with Liam right behind her. With an assist, Melinda climbed up on a stool. She waved with both hands to get everyone's attention. "Thank you all for coming. I really appreciate it, and I know Horace will appreciate it too. In a few minutes, I'm going to need you all to hide in between the bookshelves and a few of the kids can crouch down behind the checkout counter." She reached for her phone. After she read the screen, she looked out at them. "That was my lookout. It seems Horace is running a few minutes early so he will be here shortly. Everyone, hide. Remember I'll greet him and when I say, 'I heard it's your birthday,' you all jump out and say 'surprise.'"

Lainey glanced around as people rushed to find a spot to hide. "Where are we going to hide?"

Jack took her by the hand and led her over to the wall on the other side of the foyer. He leaned his shoulder against the wall and guided Lainey to stand in front of him.

"We're just going to stand here?"

"Yes."

"Everyone in their spot?" Melinda called out. After a resounding "Yes," she said, "I'm going to dim the lights."

Silence settled over the bookshop as Lainey stood there with Jack so close she couldn't help but notice the spicy scent of his cologne. It was faint but just enough to tease her senses. She breathed in deeper. Something told her she'd never smell that scent again without thinking of him.

"He's here," Melinda said as she stood behind the checkout counter.

The door creaked open, and the little bell above it jingled. The breath hitched in Lainey's lungs. She didn't make a move as the heavy footsteps sounded.

"Horace, you're here," Melinda said in a cheery voice.

"You asked me to come over." The footsteps came to a stop. "What's the matter? And why is it so dark in here?"

"Nothing is wrong. I just heard it's your birthday."

That was the cue. The lights came on as everyone including Jack and herself jumped out. "Surprise!"

Horace pressed a hand to his chest as his mouth gaped. He turned around, taking in all of their faces.

"Happy birthday." Melinda stepped around the counter and moved next to Horace.

"I...I can't believe you did all of this." Horace's weathered face broke into a smile. "Thank you." He turned around to face everyone. "Thank you all."

Everyone called out, *"Happy birthday."*

It was hard to imagine the man standing before her with a warm smile on his face and a twinkle of emotion in his eyes was once considered a Scrooge. There was happiness written all over his face and a warmth that emanated from his eyes. If this was what happened to people who belonged to the Bluestar community, well, they could just sign her up. She was totally falling in love with this small-town community.

Her gaze moved to Jack. Of course, he was the one who made this all possible. Maybe there was a bit more to her wanting to stay on the island and work at the furniture store than she was willing to admit to anyone, including herself.

Chapter Nine

SHE WAS REALLY ENJOYING herself.

Lainey was glad she had the idea to be Jack's fake date for the evening. Her gaze strayed to him. Okay, maybe this party was much better than any other she'd ever attended because her date was much better than any before him. Going forward Jack was setting a high bar for any other man after him.

Jack really was a genuinely nice guy. She still couldn't believe he'd stopped by the medical center to check on her after that accident. How did she get so lucky to have their paths cross?

There was a part of her that hoped it'd be a little longer until her memory came back—until she recalled her purpose for being on this island. She knew once her memory returned that it would mean she'd be moving on. She wasn't ready to leave the island. Not yet.

When Jack turned to her, their gazes caught and held. Her heart pitter-pattered. This wasn't supposed to be happening. She was not in a place where she was ready to become interested in someone. Although it was partly Jack's fault. He was so kind, handsome, and thoughtful. How was she supposed to resist his charms? They were quite an intoxicating combination.

"Hey, Jack," Horace said. "It's great to see you here."

The voice jolted Lainey back to her senses. She turned to find the guest of honor had joined them. While he shook Jack's hand and they greeted each other, she stood quietly by Jack's side.

Horace was about her height of five foot eight. His sparse gray hair was a little long and windswept. Scruff lined his jawline, as though he couldn't be bothered to shave. Although, his white dress shirt appeared to be pressed, and his black cardigan was in good shape.

Behind a pair of black-framed glasses, Horace's curious gaze connected with hers. "Have we met before?"

Lainey shook her head. "I don't think so. I'm Lainey Dell."

He held his hand out to her. "It's a pleasure to meet you, Lainey. I'm Horace Blackwell."

"Happy birthday."

"Thank you. I never expected such a thing. I'll tell you a secret." He leaned toward her and lowered his voice. "I've never had a birthday party."

"Really?" The word slipped past her lips before she could stop it. "Not even as a child."

Horace shook his head. "Not even then. My parents thought parties were a waste of money."

She wasn't sure what to say to that. Her parents were the exact opposite. Everything was an excuse for a party. "Well, I hope you really enjoy your party."

He nodded. "I definitely will."

They moved on so other people could speak with the guest of honor. But they couldn't move that far, because an older woman stepped in their way. *What was her name?* And then it came to her.

Mary Miller ignored Lainey and looked directly at Jack. She smiled. "Jack, it's so good to see you. I want to introduce you to my niece." And then the woman realized her niece wasn't standing next to her. Her gaze sought her out in the crowd, and she gestured for her to join them. Once the niece was next to her, she said, "Jack, I'd like you to meet Janet."

Janet looked to be a little younger than Lainey. She had shoulder-length brown hair and red-framed glasses that kept sliding down her nose. Her gaze rose to meet Jack's as she said a timid hello before lowering her gaze again. It appeared this was the blind date that Jack had told her about. Neither of the two parties seemed excited about the situation.

"It's nice to meet you, Janet." Jack was genuinely friendly, even when he was put in an awkward position. But to be fair, it didn't seem that Janet was any happier about the situation. "And I'd like you to meet my friend Lainey."

As she said *hello*, he reached over and took Lainey's hand in his. It made her heart leap into her throat. And when his fingers threaded through hers, her stomach distinctly dipped. *Oh, my.*

The older woman saw Jack take her hand. A frown formed on the woman's face. With a huff, she took her niece by the arm and moved on.

Jack let go of her hand. "Sorry about that. I panicked."

"It's okay. I don't think you were the only one. Janet didn't look very comfortable either. Just glad I could help."

"And I appreciate it."

As the crowd shifted to the side of the bookshop with the food, Lainey made her way to the other side with the shelves of books. She slowly meandered down the aisles, stopping to check out a book here and there.

She had the urge to buy a book. It'd been far too long since she'd curled up with a good book and let herself get lost in another world. Instead, her life had taken on its own adventure as she followed her mother's footsteps as laid out in the journal. She still wasn't sure what had triggered her mother to up and leave her father for this trip. There was no reason mentioned in the journal. The only thing she did know was that not long after her mother's journey concluded, she got pregnant with her.

Frustration bubbled up inside her. Why was this part of her mother's life shrouded in such secrecy? Her father insisted on changing the subject any time the past was brought up.

And now Lainey's belongings were missing. The journal—her link to the past and the secret her parents were keeping from her—was also missing. She didn't know what she was going to do without the journal.

"Lainey, are you all right?" Jack's voice drew her from her thoughts.

She blinked and then stared at him. "What?"

"Is your head bothering you? If the party is too much for you, we can go home."

She shook her head. "It's nice to get out and spend some time with people."

"But the party is over there." He pointed over his shoulder to the other side of the bookshop. "And you're over here alone and frowning like something is bothering you."

She forced a smile to her lips. She didn't want to ruin this evening for him. "Sorry. I was just enjoying the books."

Just then a chorus of "Happy Birthday" filled the room. They moved back to the other side of the bookshop. She joined in the singing and was pleased when Jack started to sing too.

For the moment, she let go of her troubles and enjoyed the party. The people of Bluestar made it easy. They were very laid back and welcoming, especially her date for the evening.

"What's your name?"

Lainey turned to find a short older woman. Her gray hair was pulled back and held in a bun. She wore large black-framed glasses from which the woman stared intently at Lainey. If the woman had said *hello*, Lainey had missed it.

"Agnes," Jack said, "this is Lainey Dell. She's visiting the island."

Agnes's brows drew together. Her gaze narrowed. "I know who you are. You're the one who got hit yesterday."

Lainey nodded. "I am."

"I'm confused." The woman's gaze swung between her and Jack. "And you two are here together?"

Jack grew quiet. His gaze lowered. What was up with him? And why was this woman so direct? Was she always like this? Or had Jack dated her granddaughter or something?

Since Jack was being unusually quiet, Lainey wondered if the friendship they'd shared and perhaps something a bit more than friendship had all been in her imagination. The acknowledgment was like a little kick to her heart. She chose to ignore the sensation.

Lainey swallowed hard. "Jack was just being nice. He's been so generous to a total stranger."

"I imagine he would be after he practically ran you down in the street."

What? Jack was the one who had hit her? *No....* That couldn't be true. There was no way. He was just being kind to her and perhaps it was because he liked her too. She needed him to deny this woman's allegation.

Lainey's gaze swung to Jack. He wouldn't look at her. *Wait.* Was this true? He was the one who hit her. How did she not know that?

She searched her memory. Everything around the accident was fuzzy. And then she recalled someone saying how sorry they were for hitting her. She could hear a voice, but she couldn't picture the face. Was it Jack? She struggled to remember. And then she recalled his vivid dark brown eyes. It was him. How had she forgotten?

"I'm sorry. I have to go." Lainey turned and headed out the door.

"Lainey, wait. Please." Jack's footsteps echoed behind her.

She didn't stop. She kept going. Why had she let herself believe he was going out of his way for her because he liked her? She was such a fool.

Tears stung the backs of her eyes. It wasn't because he'd been the one to hit her. She understood it was an accident. Sometimes she let herself get so wrapped up in her photography that she would forget about what was going on around her. Her mother used to say she had tunnel vision.

It wasn't the accident. It was the fact that she was beginning to trust him—to think he was interested in her. She'd been such a fool. He'd only been feeling guilty.

She blinked repeatedly, refusing to let him see just how much of a fool she really was. She kept walking. She had absolutely no destination in mind because she still didn't have her memory, and she didn't know where her belongings were.

A groan of frustration swelled in the back of her throat. She smothered it.

She couldn't hear Jack behind her. Was it possible he'd finally given up and turned around? She hoped so. The thought of facing him now was just too much.

She walked until she reached the beach. With it being April, the evening air was chilly. She wished she had a jacket—another thing in her missing luggage.

Her hands clenched. Another groan formed in the back of her throat and grew until it erupted from her lips. It felt as though the world was against her. Everything that could go wrong had gone wrong.

She folded her arms across her chest and rubbed her chilled arms. What was she going to do now? She was cold and getting tired. She thought of the whoopie pies Jack had for her. She was looking forward to eating them. Tears threatened to spill onto her cheeks. What was she supposed to do now? Call her father? She couldn't even do that because her phone didn't work.

Suddenly, a warm jacket was placed on her shoulders. Jack. He was still here. She wanted to shrug off his jacket, but it felt so good. As she inhaled, she was greeted with a whiff of his spicy cologne. She breathed in deeper.

She kept walking until she came upon a large boulder near the water. She climbed up onto it. Jack joined her.

For a while they quietly sat there. She stared out at the ocean as the moonlight danced upon the waves. She should say something.

She stared straight ahead. "You don't have to babysit me any longer."

"I'm not babysitting you."

"You don't owe me anything. It was an accident. That's all."

"Wait. You think I'm here because I feel guilty?"

She turned her head to look at him. "So, you don't feel guilty?"

"Of course I do. I've never had something like that happen. And I feel awful that you're having problems with your memory. I'm sorry for the accident. I thought you knew it was me that hit you."

She didn't dare tell him that wasn't what was bothering her. There was no way she was going to admit that she was starting to like him a lot. She refused to let herself be that vulnerable. She'd already had so much pain in her life.

"Well, you don't have to feel bad," she said. "I understand that it was an accident. So, you don't have to keep helping me. It's not necessary."

"You're wrong if you think I'm spending time with you out of guilt."

She turned her head to look directly at him. "Well, aren't you?"

"No." The answer was swift and firm. "I'm spending time with you because I like you. I like getting to know you."

"You do?" Her voice wavered ever so slightly.

He nodded. "I do. You're fun to be with."

"I am?" She hated how she was incapable of stringing more than two words together. But his words made her heart pitter-patter, and her thoughts became jumbled.

He smiled. "Yes, you are. You make me smile. I hope you're not leaving the island soon. I want to get to know you better."

"You do?"

He continued to smile as he once more nodded.

She really needed to say something here—something beyond two words. She swallowed hard and hoped when she spoke that her voice sounded normal. She didn't want him to know just how much he got to her.

"Well then, you're in luck."

"Why is that?"

"Because I'm not leaving Bluestar until I remember where I left my things."

"In that case would it be wrong if I hoped your memory stayed fuzzy for just a wee bit longer? Wait. Don't answer that. I shouldn't have said it. Of course, I want your memory to come back."

There was something about his discomfort that endeared him to her. He wasn't the only one who wanted to extend her visit to the island. She knew she was on a mission to uncover the truth, but she still hadn't figured out what had brought her to Bluestar. Maybe if she spent some more time looking around the island, it might spark her memory. She hoped.

He leaned toward her. The breath hitched in her lungs. Was he going to kiss her? The thought sent her pulse racing.

There was a part of her that knew starting something with him would never go anywhere. She wasn't going to stop searching for her mother's secret. She couldn't stop. Her mother thought it was so important that it was the last words she'd ever spoken.

And yet there was another part of Lainey that couldn't imagine leaving this island. Or maybe she couldn't imagine leaving Jack.

Her eyes fluttered shut. The sensation of butterflies filled her stomach as she waited to feel his lips pressed to hers. And then his lips touched her.

He kissed her cheek—a light, feathery kiss.

Her eyes opened. A sense of disappointment hit her. Her level of disappointment and confusion surprised her.

When he pulled back, she forced a smile to her lips. There was no way she was letting on the depth of her disappointment. After all, she had to stay focused on her mission and not get lost in the depths of his dreamy eyes. She had a feeling that was going to be harder than she imagined.

Chapter Ten

A CLEAN BILL OF health.

The following day Jack was happy Lainey had gotten a good report from the doctor. She still hadn't regained her memories of the day leading up to the accident, and the doctor said they might never come back. Jack felt another pang of guilt.

And he'd just heard from his sister, Josie, that they'd had someone check out early at the Brass Anchor Inn. Lainey was packing her things and relocating to the inn. He told himself he should be relieved. She was feeling better, and he could have his place back to himself. He could do his work in silence and focus on getting that promotion so he could afford to move to the city where no one knew him—where no one would try to set him up on a date.

Lainey emerged from his bedroom with a shopping bag that held her few possessions. They checked with the sheriff earlier that morning to see if her belongings had turned up yet, and the answer was the same as it had been the day before: *no*.

"Are you sure you don't want to stay?" The words crossed his lips before he could stop them.

"Thank you." She smiled at him, giving him a funny, warm sensation in his chest. "But I need to get out of your way. And now that your brother so kindly gave me a job, I can afford to get a room at the inn at least for a couple of nights. Besides, you must want your bed back." Her gaze moved to the couch. "That doesn't look very comfy."

She was right. The couch was not made for sleeping. He had a crick in his neck that he didn't think was ever going to go away.

"Since you're determined, let's go." He held his hand out for the bag in her hand.

"I can carry it. It's not heavy."

He continued to hold his hand out to her. With a sigh she handed it over. "Are you always such a gentleman?"

"It's the way my mother raised me."

"I like your mother."

"You haven't even met her." He opened the door for her. He told himself this change would be all right. After all, she was just moving to his sister's inn. It wasn't like she was leaving the island, though he knew she would be doing that soon enough.

He didn't want to get attached. Even though it was so easy to stare into her eyes. And he had almost kissed her the other night.

She had been sitting there with the moonlight highlighting her beautiful face. She'd looked so tempting. And she'd been so hurt to think he was only helping her because of his own guilt. Although that may have been his initial motive, as he got to know her, his motivation had changed.

He wanted to be her friend. Maybe if he hadn't messed up so badly in the past, he would try to pursue something more with her. But there was no undoing the past—there was no way to undo the loss of his baby—the loss of his marriage.

"Jack?" Lainey's voice drew him from his thoughts of the past.

He turned to her and had no idea what she'd just said. "What?"

Her brows drew together. "Are you all right?"

"I'm fine. Why?" Had he let his thoughts show on his face?

"Because you just walked right past your cart."

"Oh. Right." He backtracked and climbed in the cart.

And so they set off toward the inn. They were both quiet. It was a peaceful silence like two good friends that didn't feel the need to fill every second with conversation.

In no time at all, they reached the inn. His sister, Josie, was working the front desk. When she saw them come through the door, her face lit up with a warm smile. "Welcome to the Brass Anchor Inn. Lainey, it's so nice to meet you. We didn't get a chance to speak at the party. I'm Jack's sister, Josie."

"It's nice to meet you too." Lainey glanced around at the lobby. "The inn is beautiful."

"Thanks. I'd like to take all of the credit, but I've had a bunch of help with fixing it up." Josie went on to tell her about the contest the inn hosted last year to fix up some of the rooms and how their brother Kent had worked with her assistant manager, Sara Chen, to refresh the lobby.

Jack stood quietly by and let the ladies chat. He liked how Lainey was laid back and fit in. He enjoyed listening to them talk. Knowing Lainey already had a friend made him feel better about Lainey staying here. He knew his sister would take good care of her.

The two women were still chatting when the door opened, and an older couple walked in.

"I'll be right with you," Josie said before turning back to Lainey. "I've put you in a beachfront room."

Lainey pulled a small wad of cash from her pocket. Jack didn't miss the surprised look that crossed over his sister's face. In a blink, it was gone.

Josie sent him a questioning look, but before he could answer, Lainey spoke up. "I'm sorry. I had an accident, and all I have on me at the moment is cash. But I have a job now so I'll be able to pay you."

Josie, who was used to credit only, paused as though to consider the situation. Her gaze moved between Lainey and himself. "Why don't we settle up later?"

Lainey hesitated. "Are you sure? You don't even know me."

"But my brother will vouch for you?" Josie's gaze moved to him. "Won't you?"

He nodded.

"That's good enough for me." She reached behind the counter and grabbed a key. "You're in room one fifteen."

As his sister started to explain how to find the room, Jack said, "I'll show her the way."

Josie nodded before she moved on to the couple behind them.

He'd spent a lot of time in the inn since his sister had inherited half of the business. He didn't get it. She could have worked in the hotel business anywhere in the country, and yet she insisted she wanted to stay here on the island.

He was looking forward to getting away from Bluestar. When he was in the city, he'd just be another face in the crowd. No one would care about what had happened during his failed marriage. No one would notice the dark circles under his eyes when the nightmares would wake him in the middle of the night and he couldn't go back to sleep.

As he led Lainey along the hallway, he knew there was a lot he'd also miss about Bluestar, like how his siblings were always there for each other. They'd been through a lot together both good and bad. He was grateful for them.

"Jack?"

He paused and turned to Lainey. He sent her a questioning look.

She pointed to the door behind her. "Isn't that the room?"

He glanced at the room number. She was right. He'd walked right past it. He retraced his steps.

Lainey unlocked the door and stepped inside. He followed her and placed the bag on the end of a dresser. She looked around the room. The walls were painted in a pale blue. On the walls were framed black and white photographs of different locations around the island.

"Are these photos of the island?"

"Yes, they are."

"They're beautiful. I wish my camera still worked. I'd love to take some similar photos."

He thought of her broken camera. It was definitely old. He wondered if it was all she could afford or if it was some sort of nostalgia thing. The guilt over causing the accident that had destroyed her camera kept him from asking about it.

She turned to him. "I need to get a new phone, and then I'd like to see some of the sights. Can you point me in the right direction?"

He checked the time. It was almost noon. "I have a better idea. Why don't we go grab some lunch, and then I'll give you the grand tour?" He noticed how she didn't immediately jump on the idea. "Of course if you'd rather see it on your own, I totally understand."

She shook her head. "It's not that. I just feel bad about taking up so much of your time."

"Don't. I... I've enjoyed hanging out with you, and with it being Saturday, it's not like I have to work or anything." Though, he couldn't help but think about an idea he'd come up with last night to add to his proposal—the proposal that would woo his boss and get him the promotion from team leader to department manager. His salary was what was holding him back from making his move to the Big Apple. With this promotion, he'd make more money and be able to afford a very modest city apartment.

Lainey hesitated. "Are you sure you want to go sightseeing? I mean I've taken up so much of your time the past few days. I don't want to be a burden."

Was she serious? She was far from a burden. The truth of the matter was he enjoyed her company more than he was willing to admit. There was just something about her warm smile, bubbly laughter, and sparkling eyes that drew him in. He couldn't get enough of her.

But that was totally ridiculous. He hardly knew her. They weren't even suited for each other. If he were to spend more time with her, he'd come to find that they were incompatible.

With that thought in mind, he said, "You are absolutely no burden." He was certain by the end of the day, their differences would become glaringly obvious. He would learn why he would never follow through with kissing her. He cleared his suddenly dry throat. "Where would you like to eat?"

She led the way out of the room. "I don't know. What do you suggest?"

He gave it some thought. They'd already visited the Lighthouse Café. There was the Purple

Guppy Pub and Little Moon Hibachi Grille. But he was thinking they should do something different—someplace where they would be less likely to be disturbed by well-meaning and friendly passersby. And then a thought came to him.

"How do you feel about sandwiches?"

"I like them. Why?"

"Well, while you get your phone situation settled, I'll see about getting us some lunch." He waved at her to follow him. "Come on."

Chapter Eleven

She had a working phone.

Lainey expelled a big sigh of relief as she rushed out the door to find Jack waiting on the sidewalk for her. She held up her new phone. "I am back in business."

He smiled. "One problem solved."

Her thoughts turned to her lost belongings. Where were they? It was the question she'd asked herself hundreds of times. She still didn't have an answer.

As they walked, she checked her email. There was a message from her editor. She would deal with it later. Her gaze skimmed down the list of new emails. There weren't any notifications about recent purchases from her credit card company. She breathed a sigh of relief.

When she checked her voice mailbox, there were messages from her father. Lainey couldn't put that off any longer. And so, when they made it to Beachcomber Park where families were enjoying the warm springtime weather, Lainey asked Jack to give her a moment. He made his way over to the seawall.

As she walked slowly around the park, she placed the call. Her stomach knotted up. Her father didn't know she had her mother's journal or that she'd been following in her mother's footsteps. She knew if she told him that, he'd demand she stop what she was doing and come home.

She couldn't do that. She needed to see this journey through to the conclusion. Although, she feared if she didn't get her memory back, her journey would end right here.

She dialed his number. The phone rang twice.

"Elaine, are you all right?" Her father's voice was filled with uncharacteristic emotion.

Guilt assailed her. They might not agree on the path for her future, but she loved her father, and he loved her. That was never in doubt.

"Yes. I'm fine."

"Then why did my calls keep going to voicemail?"

"Because I was traveling and along the way I broke my phone. It took me a bit to find a place where I could get a new one. I'm sorry. I didn't mean to worry you."

There was a heavy sigh. "Are you coming home now?"

She hesitated because she knew another argument was about to ensue. It was the same one they'd been having for months.

"Not yet."

"Elaine, you know you have responsibilities here. I was understanding in the beginning. I knew you were struggling after your mother…" His voice faded away. He couldn't bring himself to say that her mother was dead. It was almost like he was waiting and hoping that it would all be some horrible nightmare, and her mother would be waiting at home for him. Her father cleared his throat. "But now it's time to get on with things. Business waits for no one."

"But I am working. Have you looked at my travel blog lately?" Thankfully, she'd planned ahead and had future posts already scheduled.

"Of course I did. When I couldn't reach you on the phone, I checked your site. It's the only reason I didn't send my security team out searching for you."

"I'm sorry to worry you." She meant it. "But I can't come home. Not yet. I have a few more places I want to investigate."

Her father sighed. He was quiet for a moment, as though biting back an order for her to come home right away. Instead, he said, "I really wish you would come home. The house is really empty these days."

There was a weariness in his voice that she'd never heard before. He didn't say it, but she knew he was having problems going home because her mother wasn't there waiting for him. Her mother would greet them with one of her big smiles. She'd had a gentle way of soothing her father and listening to his problems at the office.

Try as she might, Lainey was not her mother. She couldn't be there for her father the way her mother had been. Her mother used to tell Lainey that she was very much like her father. As such, she butted heads with her father quite often.

But since they'd lost her mother, her father had been more reserved. When she'd told him she was taking a leave of absence from her position as a corporate lawyer within her father's company, he'd tried to change her mind by offering her a promotion, but nothing he offered would have changed her mind.

"I wish you would come home. I..." His voice trailed off. Her father had never been good with sharing his emotions.

"I miss you too." She'd always been a daddy's girl when she was growing up.

Her thoughts turned to her mother's journal. Knowing her credit cards hadn't been stolen gave her hope that wherever she left her belongings, they were safe—for now.

They spoke for a few more minutes as he filled her in on what was going on with the company. He was poised to take control of another company. She'd worked on some of the contracts that had led up to this acquisition. In the end, her father would break the new company into pieces and sell off the profitable pieces and discard the rest.

Lainey listened, but she wasn't invested in it. Because one thing she'd finally admitted to herself was that she didn't want to move up in her father's company. It wasn't for her. She wanted something else for her future. But she hadn't made any firm decisions about what that might be.

"I'm needed for a meeting," her father said. "Please stay in touch. And don't drop your phone again."

"I won't. I promise." She had no intention of blindly stepping into a street again. But she had to admit that the one good thing that came out of it was meeting Jack. A smile pulled at her lips. "I love you."

"Me too." It was as close to an *I love you* as her father ever got.

Once she disconnected the call, she walked over to where Jack was sitting. "Sorry about that."

"Is everything all right with you and your father?"

She nodded. "He was a bit worried when he couldn't reach me. I had to explain about my broken phone."

"Did you tell him about the amnesia too?"

She shook her head. "I left out everything about the accident. I didn't want him to worry."

"I bet he was glad to hear your voice."

"He was. And I was happy to hear from him too. His sixtieth birthday is coming up in a couple of weeks. I was thinking I would go home and surprise him."

"I'm sure he would love to see you."

"I had something more than just a visit in mind. My mother used to make big deals out of milestone birthdays. I was thinking I would throw him a big party like she would have done. I know how much he misses my mother."

Jack averted his gaze. "It sounds like a good plan."

"I'll call his assistant this evening and set something up."

"Are you ready for lunch?"

Her gaze moved to the bag in his hand. "Definitely."

"Then right this way." He led her down to the beach.

Lainey smiled. It wasn't just any picnic lunch. It was lunch on the beach. And they had it on their rock—the rock where Jack had almost kissed her the other night. She stifled a sigh as she recalled how his lips had landed on her cheek instead of her lips. She hadn't realized how much she wanted him to kiss her until it didn't happen.

She wondered why he'd decided not to kiss her. Was it because he wasn't into her that way? It seemed like her timing with men was always off. If she was ready for a relationship, the guy wasn't. If a guy was ready for something serious, she wasn't. And right now, she most definitely wasn't ready to start anything.

At this point, she didn't even know where to find her belongings. She'd called the sheriff that morning, but he didn't have an update for her. She was beginning to think she was never going to locate her possessions.

"Don't you like your sandwich?" Jack's voice drew her from her rambling thoughts.

She glanced down at the uneaten Italian sub in her hands. "Sorry. I was just enjoying the view."

That was no lie. This spot on this rock was idyllic. She stared out at the ocean. The water was calm that day. The sunlight danced over the ripples in the water. In the distance was a sailboat. Its tall sail was a bright yellow. The boat gently weaved and bobbed over the water.

She imagined jumping on that sailboat and sailing away. She could leave behind the grief of losing her mother and the frustration of having holes in her memory. But she knew that was just wishful thinking. There was no out running the deep pain of loss.

"You're still not eating."

She glanced over at Jack, who only had a bite of his sandwich left. He was right. She needed to eat, and then she needed to explore this island. Maybe something would jar her memory, and she'd remember why she'd come here.

While she bit into her sandwich, Jack said, "I love this spot. And thanks to you, I have a feeling my future will include sitting here—often."

She smiled. "Glad I could help. But technically, this is my spot. I mean, after all, I did find it."

"Your spot?" He arched a brow.

"Yes. My spot."

"Are you planning to put up a plaque or something?" Though his brow was still arched, his eyes twinkled with humor.

She loved that he was willing to play along. "You know I hadn't thought of it, but now that you've mentioned it. That sounds like a good idea." She slid over so she was able to see more of the boulder they were sitting on. "Where do you think the plaque should go?"

Jack quietly considered his answer. "I don't know."

"We could put it right here." She placed her hand right between them.

"I don't think so." He leaned forward. "I think it should go right here on the front of the rock so everyone passing by the rock will see it."

"Oh, I like that idea. And it will say Lainey's Rock."

"I think it should say Jack's Rock. After all, this is my island."

Her mouth gaped. "Wait. Are you telling me that you own this whole island?"

The hint of a smile pulled at the corners of his lips. "Well, now that you mentioned it..."

She gently reached out and pushed against his shoulder. "Stop. You don't own this island."

He sighed. "Maybe I don't, but I know every inch of it, so why don't we go take a tour."

Lainey loved the idea. "Okay. It's a plan."

"But first, you have to finish your lunch."

She glanced down at the uneaten sandwich. He didn't have to tell her twice, because suddenly, she'd gotten her appetite back. She finished off the sandwich as well as the dill pickle spear that had come with it.

After they cleaned up, she asked, "Does the beach go the whole way up this side of the island?"

"No. It leads up to the inn and goes a bit further, but then it becomes very rocky and overgrown."

"Oh. Then what do you suggest?"

He paused as though to give the idea a little thought. "I think we should go to the inn. They have bicycles that the guests can use to explore the island."

"You want to go bicycling?"

"Sure." He glanced at her. "You do know how to ride a bike, don't you?"

"Um... Would you think less of me if I said no?"

The surprise showed on his face. "No. Of course not. But you can learn...if you want."

She did want to learn. It didn't appear so hard. And it looked like good exercise. "Sure."

As they made their way up the beach, he asked, "Why didn't you have a bike as a kid?"

She shrugged. "We lived in the city, and my mother said it wasn't safe. When I asked my father for one, he agreed with my mother."

"So, what did you do as a kid? Sit around and watch television?"

Lainey smiled as she shook her head. "No." She wasn't so sure she wanted to reveal her family to him. In the past, when people learned that she was Lance Devereaux's daughter, they treated her differently. She didn't want Jack to like her because of her last name. And then there was the chance that he would do what some people did and hate her because of her father's ruthless business decisions—decisions that had left many people jobless over the years.

"I'm sorry," Jack said. "I shouldn't have asked."

"No. It's fine. My parents were insistent that I keep busy. There were dance lessons and piano. When I got older, there were acting and voice lessons."

"Were these things you wanted?"

She nodded. "At first. I wasn't sure what I wanted to do when I grew up."

"And I take it that you ruled out all of those things?"

She nodded. "I was terrible at piano. My mother and I used to fight nonstop about me practicing. She wanted me to do it every day. I wanted to do it when I felt like it, and that was maybe once a week, right before my lesson."

"And the others?"

"Well, I have two left feet, so dance was an absolute disaster. My voice isn't anything special, so I was informed that I wouldn't make it professionally."

"And the acting?"

"That I was good at. And I enjoyed it."

"So, why aren't you an actress?"

"My father said acting was a nice hobby, but I needed something more serious."

"Really? And what did he have in mind?"

"I ended up going to law school." She hadn't meant to reveal that, but Jack was so easy to talk to it slipped out.

She watched his expression. He tried to hide his surprise, but his eyes gave him away.

"So, you're an attorney?"

"Not at the moment. I'm a travel writer. I have a blog and sell articles to a publisher."

"That's quite a diversion from law."

"It is. But I found I'm not good at sitting around the office all day. I like to get out and feel the sun on my face."

"And how do your parents feel about your change in career?"

"My father isn't happy about it. I'd like to think my mother would understand my decision." When she saw the confusion on his face, she said, "My mother... She, um... She passed..." It was so hard to admit this to him. A lump of emotion formed in her throat. She swallowed hard. "It was seven months ago."

Seven painful, lonely months. Finding her mother's journal had helped. She loved reading her mother's words. In Lainey's mind, she could hear her mother's voice. It was like her mother was right there with her, telling her about a period in her life. It made her feel even closer to her mother.

Lainey had read the journal over and over again. But her mother hadn't been specific in a lot of cases. There were so many abbreviations for places as well as people, so it was a puzzle that Lainey was intent on figuring out.

Jack didn't say anything in response to her painful admission. Instead, he reached out and took her hand in his own. He laced his fingers with hers and gave her hand a squeeze. The simple action gave her such comfort.

When he went to withdraw his hand, she tightened her hold on him. There was a moment where his hand froze, as though he were torn between pulling away from her and clinging to their connection. And then his fingers slipped back into their comfortable embrace of her own fingers.

They walked the rest of the way to the inn in a comfortable silence. She wondered what her mother would say about her being on Bluestar Island—about her spending time with Jack. She wanted to think her mother would understand her choices. Her father, on the other hand, didn't seem to understand anything about her.

Chapter Twelve

I T WAS A TEACHING moment...

Jack had arranged for them to borrow two bicycles from the inn, and then he showed Lainey how to ride a bike. In the beginning, she'd appeared to be unsteady and uncertain in equal parts, but he kept encouraging her to try again. And again.

There had been frustrating moments, but he refused to give up. He was certain she would figure it out. When she finally cycled the whole way around the parking lot without having to stop, the smile on her face practically beamed. His work here was done.

She rolled to a stop next to him. "I did it."

"Yes, you did. Are you sure you didn't learn how to ride when you were a kid?"

"I'm positive." Her eyes twinkled with happiness. "Thank you."

In that moment, he had an urge to reach out and draw her close. He longed to kiss her again—this time on the lips. He regretted not doing that the last time. The question was would he get another chance?

His gaze dipped to her mouth. What would she do if he were to kiss her? Would she kiss him back?

He jerked his thoughts to a halt. What was he doing? He'd already destroyed his marriage and so much more. He didn't have the right to move on and be happy.

He glanced away. "You're welcome. Are you ready to go for a ride?"

She nodded. "Yes, I am."

"Where would you like to start?"

"We could start at one end of the island and work our way to the other."

He was surprised by her eagerness. "Wow. That's a lot of ground to cover."

She frowned. "I thought this is a small island."

"I guess small is a relative term, but this island is about three miles wide and approximately nine miles long. So there's lots of ground to explore."

She paused. "I didn't realize the island was that large."

"We'll do it your way. Just so you know that there won't be enough time to explore everything today. It might take us a few days."

"I'm good with that. On Monday can we go after I finish at the store?"

He'd forgotten that she had taken his brother up on his offer for temporary help. He nodded. "We can do that. You know when I suggested the working arrangement, I had no idea you're an attorney. You don't have to work at the store. I can explain things to my brother."

She frowned at him. "Please, don't do that."

"Do what?" He was just trying to make things better for her.

"Treat me different because you learned about my past."

He opened his mouth to defend his action, but then he wordlessly closed his mouth. She began to pedal away, and he followed. He remained quiet because he didn't want to make whatever had just happened between them even worse. He was still puzzled about why she was being defensive about being an attorney.

She loved biking.

Lainey let Jack take the lead, since she had absolutely no idea where she was going. They set off at a leisurely pace toward the northern tip of the island. She loved it all: the scenery with the abundant greenery, from farms to even a Christmas tree farm. She might have to go back and investigate it further.

She inhaled the salty air as the sun warmed her face. She was definitely buying a bike. She wasn't so sure it was the safest mode of transportation in Manhattan, but who knew if she'd live there the rest of her life.

Now that she'd gotten out and explored a good portion of the country, she was rethinking everything about her future. Although, there were her friends and her father to think of. She wasn't sure she wanted to live far from them.

"Do you still want to keep going?" Jack asked. "We can turn around here."

She realized she'd gotten lost in her thoughts and was lagging behind. She picked up the speed to catch up to him. "Let's keep going. I'm really enjoying the ride. This island is so beautiful. I love how there's the town, and now there's all of this nature surrounding it. Have you lived here your whole life?"

He nodded. "Most of my immediate family lives on the island. You've already met Kent, Liam, and Josie."

"I forget. How many siblings do you have?"

"Five. There's Grant. He's a doctor on the mainland. And there's also Owen. He's the youngest in the family and a gamer."

"Wow. You have a big family. That's really nice. In my family, there's just me." She'd always wanted a sister, but her mother said it wouldn't be possible. She never elaborated on why she couldn't have more children. Every time Lainey wanted to ask why, she recalled the deep sadness that had come over her mother when she spoke of not having more children. Lainey decided to let the subject slide.

"A large family has its pluses, but sometimes I would wish I was an only child, especially when there was a long line for the bathroom. But most of the time I was grateful for my loud and crazy family."

"So, then why do you want to move away?"

He was quiet for a moment. She wasn't sure he was going to answer the question. Perhaps she shouldn't have asked it. She hadn't meant to overstep. She was just curious to learn more about him.

"As great as my family is, it's impossible to set up any sort of boundaries. And my mother is so anxious for me to meet someone special."

She wondered about this. He was certainly handsome, kind, and the perfect package. So, why was he single?

"And you don't want to date?"

He shook his head. "That part of my life is over."

Wow. That was a bold statement for someone as young as him. What could have happened to make him write off that part of his life?

She tried to be encouraging. "Maybe in time you'll change your mind."

He shook his head. "I don't think so. Not after what happened."

Well, now she needed to know what happened. But she wasn't going to ask. It wasn't her business. And yet the question ate at her. The words rushed up her throat and hovered on the tip of her tongue.

Nope. She wasn't going to do it. She swallowed hard.

"What about you?" He glanced her way. "Are you in a relationship?"

"No. My last relationship ended almost a year ago. I was always working, and he got tired of being alone. I couldn't really blame him. And then my mother got sick. It was just supposed to be the flu but she kept getting sicker until my father took her to the hospital. It all happened so fast."

It was a rhetorical question that just hung there in the silence as her heart grieved for her mother who still had so much life to live. It was so unfair that she was snatched away so soon.

It took her a moment to gather herself. Ever so softly, she admitted, "I... I still wake up some mornings and hope it was all a nightmare." Her admission didn't help make the moment any less awkward. She blinked back her unshed tears and tried to steer the conversation toward something less painful. "Anyway, I haven't been in the mood to pursue a relationship since then. What about you? Why have you given up on dating?"

She bit down on her inner lip. She hadn't meant to share all of that with him. It was something she didn't discuss with anyone. And yet it felt good to say the words aloud.

Now she waited with bated breath, wondering what had been so traumatic in Jack's past that he'd written off relationships. Would he open up to her?

Chapter Thirteen

The silence ebbed on between them.

In fact, it stretched out so long Lainey was beginning to think Jack hadn't heard her. Perhaps it was for the best. She wasn't so sure this bonding moment was for the best, because confiding in each other would only draw them closer.

And she couldn't stay on Bluestar Island forever. She'd already decided that come the end of the week, whether she retrieved her things or not, she would be moving on. Without the journal and no new clues as to the past, she would return to New York and resume her position at the company while she figured out a plan for her future. And in the meantime, she'd work on her father's birthday party.

"This is it," Jack said. "The tip of the island. The lighthouse isn't far from here, but the path is overgrown, so I don't know if you want to keep going or not."

A few weeds weren't going to stop her from seeing her first lighthouse. "Let's keep going."

"We have to walk from here." He gestured to a bunch of weeds and brush.

Here goes nothing. She followed him into the overgrowth. She just prayed there weren't any creepy crawlies in there. Just the thought sent a shiver down her spine. Thankfully, it wasn't long until they exited onto a secluded beach.

The path was overgrown with bushes with long spindly shoots and leafy trees that hid the blue sky. They had to slow down to navigate their way over the many tree roots. In single file, they continued. She had a feeling not many knew about this place.

When at last they stepped out into the sunshine, she had to blink a few times as her eyes adjusted to the brightness. And there before them was the sand and ocean.

She glanced around and spotted the lighthouse. It was impressively big. The black and white ringed tower soared up into the sky. She couldn't wait to see it up close.

But Jack didn't walk in the direction of the lighthouse. Instead, he moved down onto the beach. She followed. When he took a seat on the sand, she plopped down beside him.

"It was a day for celebrations." His voice was so soft she had to strain to hear him over the sounds of the ocean and the salty breeze. "I had just landed the job I have now. Working for Sharps Unlimited allowed me to remain on the island and travel into New York City a few times a month. It was a compromise that I was willing to take. I'd married my high school sweetheart and Nora had just learned she was pregnant. It was like the stars had aligned. We were so happy."

Lainey could imagine a happy Jack. She bet he was a wonderful husband. She noticed the little stab of jealousy. She told herself it was because she hadn't had a special relationship like that, and it had nothing to do with Jack in particular.

She remained quiet, waiting and wondering if he would share more.

"I wanted to take Nora into the city and celebrate our good fortune. I made reservations at a hotel and an expensive restaurant in New York City. It was going to be a weekend we'd never forget. Thinking back on it, I guess it was unforgettable, just not the way I had hoped." He hesitated as he stared off into the distance. "The whole weekend was out of our price range, but I wanted to splurge. Nora had been hesitant, with a baby on the way. She hadn't wanted to spend a lot of money, but I talked her into it. After all, how many times do you get pregnant with your first baby? This was huge, and I wanted to show Nora how much I loved her."

He paused as though he had gotten lost in his memories. She didn't know where this was headed, but it obviously didn't have a happy ending.

"With it being April, rain was in the forecast. I had hoped the rain would miss us, but as we drove south, the weather deteriorated. It started off as a light shower, but the further we went, the darker the sky grew. Before I knew it, the wind was pushing against the car, and the rain came down in sheets. Nora was begging me to turn around, but I couldn't. I could barely see out the windshield. The next thing I knew, the car was hydroplaning, straight into a tree."

Lainey smothered a gasp. She willed him to say that the mother and baby had survived. When he didn't say anything, she imagined the worst.

After what felt like forever, Jack said, "Luckily, the airbags deployed, and Nora appeared to be all right. It's what I had prayed for. She tried to reassure me that it was an accident and that we were all right. I wanted to believe her. I really did. And then... Two days later... She... She had a miscarriage."

The raw agony in his voice tore at her heart. She couldn't even imagine the pain they'd endured at losing something so precious.

"I'm sorry." She knew the words were totally inadequate to convey her sympathy, but they were the best she had in the moment.

They continued sitting there. The sea breeze swept past them, but she could no longer appreciate the beauty surrounding her. Her thoughts were focused on Jack and his tremendous loss.

She had questions, but it wasn't appropriate. The fact he'd shared something so deeply personal warmed a spot in her chest. She had a feeling their friendship would endure her return to the city. When she was back in New York or wherever she eventually ended up, she imagined they'd message each other every now and then. She wanted to think the messages would be frequent, but she didn't want to set herself up for disappointment.

"After the baby..." Jack's voice was laced with pain. "Everything changed. I couldn't stop blaming myself. Even when the doctor said there could be any number of reasons for the loss, I just couldn't stop thinking that if I hadn't been so insistent we go into the city that Nora would still be pregnant."

Lainey wanted to say something here that would agree with the doctor, but she didn't think it would matter to Jack. The guilt was visible in the deep frown lines on his face. He carried around that pain with him every day. She had some idea what that was like because the grief over her mother's untimely death was the burden she carried around with her.

She leaned over to him and rested her head on his shoulder. She wrapped her arm over his broad shoulders. "I'm so sorry."

He reached up and squeezed her hand. "After the baby, our marriage began to crumble. Nora tried to tell me it wasn't my fault, but I could never really hear her. I became quiet and withdrawn. Eventually, she couldn't bear to live with me, not that I could blame her. I was in a deep funk for a long time. She moved to Boston and filed for divorce. I'd failed both her and our baby."

What was one to say to that very painful confession? Lainey's heart ached for him—for them. And now she knew why this great guy was unattached and wanting a fake date for the birthday party. It certainly wasn't the reason she'd been expecting.

"Anyway that's my story." He got to his feet. "You're probably sorry you asked."

She stood. "I'm not. Thank you for trusting me with your truth."

The muscles of his throat visibly moved as he swallowed. "Now on with the tour. This is the northern tip of the island."

"This is beautiful." It was like a secret cove. Her gaze strayed back to the lighthouse. "Does the lighthouse have a name?"

"Breakers Point Lighthouse."

"Does it still work?"

He shook his head. "It hasn't been maintained in many years. I don't think it's worked since I was a little kid."

"That's a shame."

As she continued to stare at it, she had the feeling she'd seen it before, but that was impossible. She'd never been to the island before. Still, there was something about it that was familiar to her. She was certain with time the answer would come to her.

"Can we go closer?"

"Sure. I guess. It's private property, so I don't think we can go inside or anything."

Lainey nodded her head and started toward it. She was drawn to the lighthouse. It was farther away than she'd thought. And the way was littered with rocks and weeds, not that any of it would deter her.

"Hey, slow down," Jack called out to her.

She didn't want to slow down. She felt drawn to this lighthouse. The feeling grew stronger, the closer she got to it.

When they reached the lighthouse, she was impressed by the sheer size of it. "Does someone live here?"

He shook his head. "The owner lives in town."

"What's the owner's name?" She was hoping it would jar a memory.

"Maude Clemmons. She's a widow and has lived on the island her whole life. I think the lighthouse has been in her family for generations."

The name didn't ring any bells. Still, there was something familiar about the lighthouse. She tried to walk the whole way around it, but it was impossible because the one side was nothing but a drop off littered with huge boulders that waves beat against.

"Maybe we could take a peek inside."

Jack reached out and caught her arm. "Lainey, don't."

She turned to him. "Why not?"

He pointed to the old, weathered sign that read: *Do Not Trespass*.

She wanted to ignore it. She had the feeling if she kept searching, she would gain the answers to her questions. Lately, all she'd had were questions, and she was so anxious for the answers.

"All I want is a closer look." Before he could stop her, she vaulted over the old wood fence that had seen its better days.

"This is a bad idea," he called out from behind her.

She heard his footsteps behind her. She waited for him to stop her, but surprisingly, he didn't this time.

The ground leading to the lighthouse was rocky and uneven. It took some concentration to navigate the rugged terrain.

After she worked her way a quarter of the way around the lighthouse, she found an old footpath that led to a black wood door.

Her hand reached out for the doorknob. Jack reached out, stopping her. "Don't."

With a sigh, she acknowledged he was right. She nodded her head and backed away. She couldn't just go barging into the little house-like structure at the base of the lighthouse.

Why did this lighthouse call to her? And then it came to her. It reminded her of an old photo in the back of her mother's journal. But could this be the same lighthouse?

Her mind said that the chance of this being the same exact lighthouse was slim to none. But her heart said there was a possibility, and that was better than none. However, she would never know the answer if she didn't remember where she'd left the journal.

And then recalling her phone, she pulled it out of her pocket. She wanted to document this place. If nothing else, she could use the images for a new article.

"I just want to get some photos."

Jack stepped back as she snapped some close-up shots. He must have thought there was something wrong with her by the way she was drawn to this place. But there was something special about it.

After she took a couple dozen photos, including some shots of the wildflowers around the base of the lighthouse, they started back toward the beach. She would stop every now and then to turn around and take another photo.

"Don't you think you have enough photos yet?" Jack arched a questioning brow.

"It isn't the amount of photos. It's having the right one from the right angle with the right amount of light."

"And how do you know when you have the right one?"

"When it speaks to me."

"Speaks to you? What does it say to you?" He watched her intently, as though he were truly interested in her response.

She shrugged. "It depends. Sometimes the photo will speak to the history of the subject. Sometimes it will evoke an emotion in someone. Other times it will say 'come visit me.' And if I have a very special shot, it will say all of those things."

"Who knew photos could say so many things? If I didn't know better, I'd say you were a professional photographer."

She shrugged. "I took some photography classes while I was in college. I've been taking pictures since I was a kid. I would fill photo albums with snapshots."

"Why didn't you become a professional photographer?"

She shrugged. "Being the only child, there was a lot of pressure for me to follow in my father's footsteps."

"And so you got your law degree?"

She nodded. "I specialize in contract law."

"And yet you're here taking photos instead of being in the office reviewing contracts. Maybe that should tell you something."

She shook off the idea. "I can't just give up on my career to do something I enjoy."

He stopped walking and turned to her. "Did you hear what you just said? If your heart isn't in law, you need to make a change. Life is too short to keep doing something out of some sense of obligation, if it doesn't bring you happiness."

She didn't like that he was turning her words around on her. If she didn't stay the course, who would take over the company some day for her father? Who would one day run LMD Inc.?

When she glanced at him, he sent her an expectant gaze. Feeling vulnerable and not ready to face the multitude of emotions tied up in her future, she said, "This from the man who is planning to pick up and move away from this island that you obviously love and the family you care about to move to the city. Do you even know anyone there?"

He paused as though letting the weight of her words sink in. "Well, if you return to New York, I will know you."

"That's not what I mean." She sighed. "Running away from your problems won't fix them. They will just follow you."

"You sound like you're speaking from personal experience."

She was, but she wasn't ready to admit it. Instead, she headed for the rugged path that led back to their bikes. The trek was quiet as each of them were lost in their own thoughts.

When she made it to the clearing, she moved to her bike and picked it up. "Ready to head back to town?"

As she pedaled, she thought about their conversation. Was she running away from something? Or running toward something?

For so long, she'd told herself she was running toward the truth—toward the secret her mother tried to tell her on her deathbed—the secret that her father refused to speak of.

But now Jack had her wondering if she was also running from the expectations that awaited her back in Manhattan. After experiencing this adventure and capturing it through the lens of her camera and then sharing the beauty of this country with the world, would she be able to go back to dealing with black and white legal jargon? Would a monochrome existence be enough for her?

Chapter Fourteen

Alone again.

Sunday came with blue skies and glorious sunshine. Tux sunned himself in the window. Meanwhile, Jack sat staring at the blinking cursor on his monitor. He'd meant to go over his presentation once more to see if he'd missed anything, but he was distracted.

He kept checking his phone every few minutes in case he'd missed Lainey's phone call. So far he hadn't heard a word from her. He couldn't decide if that was a good thing or not.

He was still surprised he'd opened up to her about his marriage and the baby. He hadn't even told his family about the baby. They'd been waiting until the end of the first trimester before they told anyone. It wasn't that long to wait because Nora hadn't realized she was pregnant until she was nine weeks along.

After they'd lost the baby, he just didn't have the heart to tell them. He thought maybe Nora would mention it to the family, but she hadn't brought it up either. Maybe if they had, it would have helped ease the guilt that weighed on him.

Maybe it would have helped save his marriage. He would never know.

On the bike ride back to town yesterday, Lainey had been quiet—too quiet. He'd noticed she appeared to be lost in her own thoughts. When he'd tried to speak to her, he'd only gotten one- or two-word answers.

He was still hung up on the fact that she thought his plan to move to the city would be a mistake. Since she lived in New York City, he thought she would be cheering him on to make the big move.

Maybe it had nothing to do with his plan. Maybe it was her way of letting him know that even if they were in the same city, this thing—whatever you wanted to call it between them, friendship or perhaps something a little more—wouldn't continue. This was her way of letting him down gently.

No matter what she said, it wouldn't change his mind. Whether they saw each other again or not, he was moving. He'd failed as a husband. He'd failed as a father. And now he was failing as a son because he was never going to have the perfect family that his mother wished for him. Once he moved, he wouldn't have to see the disappointment in his mother's eyes.

Buzz-buzz.

He reached for his phone. It was Lainey. He noticed how his heart sped up.

"Hi. Are you busy?"

"No." His gaze moved to the computer screen. "Not at all. What do you need?"

"I was just wondering if we could continue our tour of the island."

She was still interested? "Sure. I can meet you at the inn in fifteen minutes. Would that work for you?"

"It sounds perfect."

After he hung up the phone, Tux stood up and stretched. He made his way over to Jack's desk and rubbed his head against Jack's chin. Tux let out a loud purr.

Jack's fingers moved over the keyboard as he shut down the computer. "I'm sorry, buddy. You're on your own today. I have a date."

He was struck by the last word. He thought about it for a moment and then decided he was okay with this being a date.

With the computer off and a last pat for Tux, he rushed to the bathroom to freshen up before he left. And then he was out the door, anxious to see Lainey again. He hoped things would go better today. He'd definitely stay away from the heavy subjects. Just light conversation and good times.

When he reached the hotel, Lainey was standing on the porch, waiting for him. When she smiled at him, he felt his heart thump-thump. He had the immediate urge to go up to her and take her into his arms. It was like her smile was the sun, and he was being drawn into her gravitational pull.

When he bounded up the steps, she brushed past him. "You don't have to go inside."

He turned around to find her next to two bicycles. "You already signed out the bikes?"

"I did. Let's go. Maybe we could get some lunch."

"Uh... Sure." He told himself that any time they spent together was fine with him.

As they made their way into town, they talked about where they should have lunch. He liked the idea of having another picnic on the beach. This time he wouldn't resist a chance to kiss her. But Lainey appeared interested in trying another of the restaurants in town. He could deal with that.

He was just about to give Lainey her choice of places to eat when he noticed Birdie frantically waving at them from the sidewalk. It wasn't a wave of greeting. No. This was a wave like she had something important to tell them. He was almost afraid to find out what she wanted. With Birdie, it could be anything from a nugget of gossip to involvement in some outlandish scheme.

"I think that woman is trying to get your attention." Lainey slowed down.

"That's Birdie. She's a really nice lady. I guess we should see what she wants."

They guided their bikes over to the other side of the road. Birdie's face lit up with a friendly smile. "Hi."

"Hi," he said. "Birdie, I'd like you to meet Lainey Dell." He looked at Lainey. "And, Lainey, this is Birdie Neill."

"We've met." Birdie sent Lainey a concerned look. "I heard you had an accident. How are you doing?"

"I'm good." Lainey reinforced her words with a smile.

"I'm so glad to hear that." Birdie rushed on. "I was hoping you two could help me out."

"What do you need?" Jack knew Birdie's requests could be as small as walking her dog or big as taking over organizing some town function. His gut tightened as he awaited her next words.

"I need you two to run the three-legged race at Spring Fling this coming weekend. I've been working to organize it with Hannah Bell, um, I mean Walker. It's going to take me a while to get used to her new last name." Birdie's gaze turned to Lainey. "I'm so glad you decided to stick around the island. I just knew you were going to love it here."

Lainey's brow scrunched up. "You said we met before, but I'm having some memory problems. Did we meet at the birthday party?"

Birdie shook her head. "I couldn't make it to the party. You really can't remember?"

Lainey shook her head. "The accident caused me to have some short-term memory loss."

Birdie nodded in understanding. "We met on the ferry from the mainland. You were taking photos and seemed to have something on your mind."

"Did I happen to have a suitcase and a purse with me?"

Birdie nodded. "I'll never forget that purse. It was almost as big as you."

Lainey smiled as tears shimmered in her eyes. "It is big. It was my mother's. Do you... Do you know where it is?"

Birdie shook her head. "We parted ways when we got off the ferry. And I don't know where you were headed."

"Oh." The smile fled Lainey's face.

Jack could feel her disappointment. It was so profound. She looked as though she'd just lost her last chance to find her belongings. He desperately wanted to help her, but he didn't know what to do.

He reached over and took her hand in his. As he laced his fingers with hers, he noticed how right it felt. His gaze moved to her. "At least we know your things are somewhere on the island."

Her gaze was lowered when she nodded her head. "I guess so."

Jack turned to Birdie. It wasn't a good idea to include Lainey in the plans for the Spring Fling. He didn't want Lainey to feel even more obligated to extend her stay on the island.

Before he could get the words out of his mouth, Agnes Dewey came rushing up the walk. "Have you heard the latest?"

Birdie expelled an exasperated sigh. She turned to them. "Thank you for agreeing to help out. I'll be in touch with the details."

Wait. They never actually agreed to this. When he turned a questioning gaze to Lainey, she shrugged.

In the background, he could hear Agnes complain. "This is going to mess up the egg decorating contest."

Everything with Agnes was a disaster. When they were about to pedal off, Birdie turned to them. "Wait. I just remembered." She looked at Lainey. "I don't know if this will be of any help, but I remember after seeing that giant purse and the suitcase you were pulling, I suggested you might want to put them in a locker at the harbor. I don't know if you followed through with the idea or not. Like I said, we parted ways as soon as we got off the ferry. It was very busy that day."

Lainey's face lit up with hope. "Thank you. That must be it."

He looked at her. "Do you remember?"

Lainey shook her head. "I don't. I'm beginning to think those memories will never come back to me, but this has to be the reason my things haven't shown up anywhere else." Lainey turned back to Birdie. "Thank you so much. You don't know how much this means to me."

"You're quite welcome." Birdie smiled while Agnes continued to frown. Jack was pretty sure the frown Agnes wore was just her normal resting face. He didn't know if he'd ever seen the woman smile.

Lainey took off on her bike. He had to pedal quickly to catch up to her.

"Do you even know where you're going?" he asked.

"Not exactly. I know the harbor is on the westward side of the island."

"Slow down. You can't get your suitcase on your bike."

Lainey slowed to a stop. "I don't want to backtrack to the inn. It's on the opposite side of the island." Her eyes lit up. "Your place isn't far from here. Could we leave the bikes there and take your cart?"

He hesitated. And yet when he looked into her eyes—the way she silently pleaded with him—he felt his hesitancy melting away. "We can do that."

He had a feeling this discovery was going to change everything for Lainey. While he was happy she would get her belongings back, he was worried she might decide to leave the island right away. He wasn't ready to say goodbye. Not yet.

Things were coming together.

Lainey was so excited to get her belongings back. When they arrived at the harbor office, she ran to the door. She rushed inside. Lucky for her there was no one standing in line.

"Do you have my stuff?"

The woman behind the counter gave her a strange look. "First, I'll need your ID."

Lainey fished it out of her pocket and handed it over. The woman typed something on the computer. It was all Lainey could do to stand there quietly.

"Your things are in locker fifty-four. It's marked in the file that you were supposed to be back for them on Saturday."

"I'm sorry about that. I had an accident."

"Well, there will be an additional day's rent plus a penalty."

"That's fine." Lainey would pay anything to get the journal back.

She was escorted to the locker area. As soon as the locker was open, she searched her suitcase. Her fingertips touched the soft leather of her mother's journal. She pulled it to her chest and breathed a sigh of relief.

When she returned to the front of the office with the huge bag slung over her shoulder and rolling her suitcase behind her, she couldn't stop smiling. Once they were back in the cart, she said, "Would you mind if we skip the sightseeing today?"

"Um, yeah. Sure. That's fine." Disappointment reflected in his eyes.

"I'm sorry. Can I have a raincheck for tomorrow?"

"We both work."

"That's right. We could get together after work. Would that work?"

He nodded. "It sounds like a plan."

He dropped her off at the inn. He told her not to worry about the bikes. He'd see that they were returned. She thanked him and headed inside.

She race-walked into the lobby. She had to know if the photo of the lighthouse in the back of the journal was the same as the one on her phone. Or, was she trying to make a connection that didn't exist?

Josie was working behind the front desk when Lainey rushed in the door. Josie smiled and waved. Any other time Lainey would have stopped to talk, but today she forced a smile to her lips, waved, and kept walking.

When she was at last in her room, she lifted the suitcase onto the bed. She unzipped it and once more pulled out the worn brown leather journal. She untied the cord around it and opened it to the back, where her mother had glued an envelope that held various pictures. She pulled them all out and sifted through them until she located the one of the lighthouse. She reached for her phone and selected the photo she'd taken the day before. She placed them side by side. The breath caught in her lungs as her gaze shifted back and forth. She looked at every detail.

It's the same one!

The pent-up breath rushed from her lungs. She'd at last located the source of one of the pictures. She hoped it would lead her to the answers about what her mother had been trying to tell her. It was still a long shot, but it was the only chance she had.

Lainey took the journal and curled up in a comfy chair near the sliding glass doors. She opened the journal and began to read. She hoped this new discovery would shed more light on the cryptic passages...

I just couldn't stay in that house a minute longer. The silence was deafening. And I felt like I might lose my mind. LD doesn't understand the desperation I feel, and I don't know how else to explain it to him.

I've tried repeatedly, and all we ever do is end up in an argument.

Hopefully, this time apart will help both of us. My therapist said journaling might help. I'm not sure about it, but I'm willing to give it a try.

I don't have a destination in mind. My first stop is in Williamsburg, VA. It is so beautiful there, like walking through the pages of a book. I took pictures. Lots of pictures. Probably more than I should have. But for a moment, while I was concentrating on the images in front of me, I wasn't thinking of the problems in my own life...

Chapter Fifteen

BEEP. BEEP. BEEP.

Monday morning, the annoying alarm on her phone woke her. Lainey found herself still in the chair with the journal pressed to her chest. She must have fallen asleep reading. Sadly, she still hadn't been able to piece together what had been troubling her mother so much that she'd left her dad and set off on a cross-country journey.

Knowing that today was her first day of work at the Turner Furniture store, Lainey headed for the shower. Now that she had her belongings back, she didn't *have* to work at the store. But she'd given her word, and Kent had been nice enough to give her a break, even though he didn't know her. That said a lot about him, and she intended to honor their agreement. Besides, she liked Bluestar Island, and this would give her a chance to meet more of its residents.

On her way to work, she stopped by the front desk. Josie was there again. And Lainey felt guilty for not stopping to speak to her the night before.

After she produced her credit card to cover the room charge, she asked if she could borrow a bike for the day. Josie agreed. Lainey pulled up the photo of the lighthouse on her phone. "Do you know who owns the lighthouse?"

Josie smiled. "So you've visited Breakers Point?"

"I did. Jack took me."

"Did he tell you that it's private property?"

"He did. I fell in love with it as soon as I saw it and had to get a closer look. That's why I'd like to know who owns it." Jack had told her the other day, but she couldn't recall the name. When Josie hesitated, Lainey said, "I write a travel blog, and I thought the lighthouse might make a good subject for an article." It was no lie. It just wasn't the whole truth.

Josie seemed to accept her explanation. "It's owned by Maude Clemmons."

"Does she live on the island?" After Josie nodded, Lainey asked, "Could you give me her address?"

After making a note of the location on her phone, she said, "Thank you so much. I better get going. I don't want to be late for work."

"Work? I thought you were on vacation."

"I am, but Kent needed some help at the store, and at the time, I needed some cash. Anyway, I said I'd help out this week, and I don't want to be late. I'll see you later."

As Lainey walked away, she had a feeling Josie would be calling her brother for a better explanation. Lainey climbed onto the bike and was disappointed to find she didn't have time to seek out Maude Clemmons before work.

The morning dragged out as she kept checking the time. Kent had been great at explaining things to her. And any time a customer had a question she couldn't answer, Kent was there to handle things. She was surprised at how busy the store could be. She also noticed how the stream of customers ebbed and flowed. Sometimes six customers would come through the door, one right after the other. Other times an hour could pass with not one customer.

At lunchtime, Sara showed up with lunch. Lainey couldn't be rude and walk out after Sara had gone out of her way to include Lainey. She found she really enjoyed getting to know Sara and Kent. It was a bit surprising to see how much Jack had in common with his older brother. They had some of the same mannerisms, and they resembled each other. Though she couldn't deny that Jack was the more handsome of the two.

After they ate, Lainey asked Kent if she could run out for a quick errand. He didn't have any problem with it. She rushed to Maude's house. It was a modest sunny-yellow house with robin's-egg blue shutters. It definitely reminded Lainey of an island house.

Her stomach knotted up as she walked to the door. Would this lead her to an answer? Or more questions?

She rapped her knuckles on the door and waited. When there was no answer, she knocked harder.

"There's no one home."

Lainey turned to see the neighbor lady standing on her front porch with a little brown dog by her side. She was tall and slender. Her dark hair was pulled back in a ponytail. In her right hand, she held a coffee mug that read: *Dog Mom*.

Lainey raised her voice. "I was really hoping to speak to Maude. Do you know when she'll be back?"

The woman's brows drew together. "Are you a relative or something?"

"No. I wanted to discuss the lighthouse with her."

"Oh. She still owns the Breakers Point. But if you're thinking of buying it, I wouldn't. It needs a lot of work."

"Thanks. Do you know when she'll be back?"

The woman took a sip of coffee. "Well, she went to the mainland for a doctor's appointment and to visit with friends. She won't be back until Friday."

Worried that there might be something wrong with Maude for her to travel to the mainland for medical treatment, she asked, "Is Maude all right?"

"Sure, she is. It's just a regular checkup."

"Oh." She was confused about why Maude would travel to the mainland just to see a doctor when there was already one on the island.

"You aren't from around here, are you?"

"No, I'm not."

"Well, there isn't much medical care on the island aside from the medical center. If you need to see a specialist or are in need of diagnostic testing, you have to go to the mainland. But she'll be back on Friday because she won't want to miss Spring Fling."

That reminded Lainey that she had to talk to Jack about what they needed to do for the event. She'd ask him when they got together after work.

After thanking the woman for the help, she hurried back to the furniture store. She was disappointed that Maude wasn't home. But Friday wasn't that far away. Just a few more days and maybe she'd gain some answers. She hoped.

The best Monday...

Jack couldn't stop smiling after Lainey had called, and he'd invited her to dinner. She hadn't even hesitated when she'd accepted his invitation. At six o'clock, they met up at the Purple Guppy Pub.

Lainey was waiting on the sidewalk for him. She was all smiles. It warmed a spot in his chest. He couldn't help but smile back at her.

He stopped in front of her. "I take it your first day at the store went well."

"It did. I really enjoyed myself. Your brother is very kind, and I got to meet a lot of people."

"You better be careful or you're going to fall in love with Bluestar and never leave this island."

"I think you might be right." She sent him a teasing smile.

Thanks to his brother, he still had some more time to sway her into staying. Although, now that she'd found her things, she didn't need the job.

The thought deflated his mood like a balloon with a slow leak.

Once they were inside and seated, he said, "You know you don't have to keep working at the store. I can just explain to Kent that you found your belongings."

"No. Don't do that. I like working there. And it's only for one week."

He arched a brow. "You're serious?" When she nodded, he said, "Okay. I just don't want you to feel obligated. I know you have to deal with that at home."

"Oh no. Working at the furniture store isn't anything like getting a law degree in order to work in my father's company."

"Do you really dislike being an attorney?"

She paused, as though to give the question some thought. "It's not that I hate it. It's more like I don't love it. But I don't want to talk about that now."

The server showed up at their table to take their drink order. At the same time, they ordered burgers and fries.

As soon as the server walked away, Lainey rooted through her giant purse. She pulled out a black and white photo. She placed it on the table in front of him. It was an image of a lighthouse. Then she reached for her phone and pulled up a photo of the Breakers Point Lighthouse. She placed them side by side.

Her gaze met his. "What do you think?"

He glanced down at the photographs. "They are beautiful. Did you take both of them?"

She shook her head. "Do you think they are photos of the same lighthouse?"

As he compared the two photos, he could feel Lainey's gaze boring into him. What did she want the answer to be?

He swallowed hard, hoping he had the right answer. "I think they are the same." Then he pointed to one of the photos. "See this here. They both have the same missing piece."

She turned the photos around to study them. "You're right."

A smile lifted the corners of her lips and lit up her eyes. He loved when she smiled that way. She was so beautiful. The most beautiful woman in the world.

He reached out, covering her hand with his. "I hope this helps you."

Her gaze moved to their hands. He wondered if she'd pull away, but she didn't. Her gaze rose to reach his. His heart beat faster. Did she feel energy coursing between them? It made his heart beat faster.

He turned his hand over, wrapping his fingers around her hand. His thumb stroked the smooth skin of the back of her hand.

"I... I don't know." She hesitated, as though she were having a problem stringing her thoughts together. Her gaze moved to their hands and then back to his gaze. "Um... The photo was in my mother's journal. What do you think this means?"

He used his other hand to pick up the photo and turn it over. "There's no date or documentation. Do you think your mother took the photo?"

"I can't help but believe that's the case." She pulled her hand from his. She reached back into her big black purse and pulled out a brown leather book. She placed it on the table between them. "She set off on a cross-country trip before I was born. She took photos as she visited different places. Now I know she was here on the island." She flipped open the journal to one of the pages in the back. "See this." She turned it so he could read it. Her finger pointed to the initials BS. "My mother always used initials. Sometimes it could be frustrating. I didn't know if BS was a person or place. Now I'm certain it stands for Bluestar. I just don't know why she was here. But after she stopped here, there were no more entries in the journal. Does that mean she got the answers she sought?"

He looked at her and shrugged. "I don't know."

"I think my father knows, but every time I bring up the past to him, he shuts down."

He felt sorry for her. "What if you told him that you found the photo? Would he fill in the blanks?"

"He would find a way to stop me from uncovering the truth."

Jack was a little taken aback. His family could meddle, but when it came down to it, they were there for one another. "Maybe you should try talking to him again."

"Maybe." She didn't sound like she planned to take his suggestion.

Their food was delivered. Jack made the effort to change the subject. They talked about his work and the project he was working on with the hope of getting a promotion. It was the key to making his move to the Big Apple.

She loved the evening.

Lainey loved the way Jack listened to her. He wasn't just pacifying her; he appeared to care about what she said. He didn't brush off her concerns and suspicions. He listened and did his best to give her good advice.

The more time she spent with Jack, the closer she felt to him. And that just made it so much worse. Because while he was telling her about his big plans for a promotion and his move to the city, he'd also dropped the name of the company he worked for. She recognized the name of the company. And she'd suddenly lost her appetite.

She'd worked on the paperwork for her father's company to take over the business Jack worked for. Here Jack was going on about how proud he was of his project, and she knew sooner rather than later, the company he worked for would no longer exist.

She longed to warn him, but confidentiality prevented her from doing it. She knew something this volatile could easily blow up in her face. She would be brought up before the bar and her law license suspended. She couldn't do that. She hated being in this horrible position.

Thankfully, it was the end of their meal, and Jack didn't make a big deal out of her not finishing her burger or fries. Afterward, they made their way to Birdie's house. They talked about the upcoming Spring Fling. Birdie gave them the sign-up sheets with the entrants' names and ages for the three-legged race. They were also in charge of making a big sign and sorting through the burlap sacks and making any necessary repairs.

Lainey was thankful Jack had driven his cart. After their meeting, Birdie gave them a big stack of burlap sacks to take with them.

Lainey wasn't ready to go back to her room. Her mind was racing, and she wasn't ready to say goodnight to Jack. So, when he suggested they go to the beach, she readily agreed.

He parked near the seawall. They made their way down to the beach. There were a few other couples walking in the moonlight.

"I love it here," she said. "It's so calming."

"Maybe you should move here?"

The question stopped her in her tracks. "You aren't serious, are you?"

He shrugged. "Why not? You like it here. And I like you here."

Her gaze searched his. "You do?"

"I most certainly do." He reached out and tucked a strand of hair behind her ear. "I don't know if you noticed, but I've gotten used to having you around. And I'd like to have you around for a lot longer."

"But..." She was having a problem stringing her thoughts together with him so close to her. "But you're moving."

"That's true." His voice was soft as his fingers caressed her cheek. "But plans could change."

His gaze dipped. Was he thinking about kissing her? Her heart beat louder. It echoed in her ears. She'd told herself that their almost-kiss had been a one-off. They'd let themselves get caught up in the moment again. She'd been wrong.

As he leaned in to her, her eyes fluttered shut. The breath hitched in her lungs. Was this really going to happen? Was he really going to kiss her? She willed him to do it. She'd never wanted anything more in her life.

And then his warm lips were there, pressing to hers. In that moment, she let herself enjoy the kiss. She wasn't worried about secrets or jobs. Right now, her world shrank until it was just him and her.

She leaned into him. Her hands landed on his muscled chest. Beneath her fingertips, she could feel the beat of his heart. She wondered if it was beating as fast as her own.

Her hands slid up over his shoulders. Her fingers raked up through his thick hair. It felt so good beneath her fingertips. She could get used to this—very used to this. She enjoyed having him in her life—more than she was willing to admit to herself.

When he pulled back. He smiled at her. "Was that convincing enough?"

"Huh?" Her mind was already replaying that sizzling kiss. She blinked and focused on him.

His smile broadened. "I was just wondering if that kiss convinced you to consider moving to the island permanently."

She liked the way his mind worked. "I don't know." She stared up at him. She could get lost in those gorgeous eyes. "I might need some more convincing."

He let out a chuckle as he turned and held his arm out to her. She placed her hand in the crook of his arm, and then they set off down the moonlit beach in a comfortable silence.

Chapter Sixteen

Sweet dreams.

The next morning, Lainey woke up with a smile on her face. After silencing the alarm, she leaned back on the pillow and closed her eyes. She hoped to regain the dream of Jack as he held her in his arms. The image made her heart flutter. And then the very sweet image dissipated. Try as she might, she wasn't able to recreate it. With a resigned sigh, she got out of bed.

She thought of Jack on her way to the furniture store. It took all of her effort to concentrate on her work. But when there were no customers to help, her mind strayed back to Jack and their walk on the beach—hand in hand, and then there was the part where they were lip to lip. The memory caused her heart to flutter in her chest.

At lunchtime, she did the one thing she'd been avoiding—calling her father. She was upset with him for not being honest with her about the secret her mother had been keeping, but her need to try to help Jack overrode her anger with her father.

After one ring, her father's voice boomed through the phone. It was like he was sitting by the phone, waiting for her call. "Elaine, are you coming home?"

She inwardly groaned. He was forever asking her the same question. And so, she gave him the same answer she'd given him since she'd started this adventure. "Not yet."

A distinct silence ensued. "I won't waste my breath trying to convince you otherwise. So, what can I do for you this morning?"

It was sad that their relationship had been reduced to this. Once upon a time, they'd been close. She missed those times.

She swallowed. There was no way to ease into the conversation. "I... I was wondering how things are going with the Sharps deal."

"Why would you want to know that?"

"Because it was one of the last projects I worked on. I wanted to follow up on it."

"It seems strange after all the months you've been away from the business that you haven't asked about any facet of it. So, why now?"

She inwardly groaned. She should have known her father wouldn't make this an easy conversation. "If you must know, I've met someone that works for the company."

"And..."

"And I've never seen the effect of your business decisions from this side of the desk. There are good people that are going to be out of work if the deal goes through."

"Since when have you gone so soft?"

"I'm not soft." The response was automatic, but she didn't see how being soft was a flaw. "I'm compassionate."

"It doesn't matter. The deal is finalized. The announcement will be made later this week."

She wanted to ask her father to find room in his company for Jack, but to do that would open an entire can of worms, including alerting him to her location. She couldn't let that happen. She couldn't risk her father meddling and keeping her from the answers she felt were almost in reach. She hoped when Maude Clemmons returned that she might have some of those answers.

They quickly wrapped up their conversation. Just as she disconnected the phone, Jack rang. He had arranged for them to use his mother's sewing machine to sew the ripped seams in the burlap sacks. With everything that had happened in the last twenty-four hours, she'd totally forgotten about their part in Spring Fling.

Jack informed her that his mother was out of town, and he had no idea how to operate a sewing machine. He asked if she knew how to work one. She assured him that she'd learned to work a sewing machine in school. She'd helped make costumes for their Christmas play. She'd been hoping for the lead role. She ended up with a lesser role.

They'd made plans for him to pick her up after she was done working. On the way to his parents' house, they'd pick up dinner at the Pizza Pie Shoppe. It sounded like a really nice evening. She was looking forward to seeing Jack again. It felt like forever since they'd been kissing on the beach the night before.

He could get used to this.

The following day, Jack couldn't remember the last time he'd smiled this much. It had been before the car accident that had changed his life so dramatically. Honestly, he could hardly remember being happy. He knew he was; he just couldn't latch onto that buoyant feeling like he felt today.

The night before they'd made repairs to the burlap sacks. Who knew it could be so much fun? Of course, he was relegated to inspection and folding duty. Lainey did all of the sewing. She'd said it was safer for his fingers that way. He couldn't argue.

He had been impressed at how easily she worked the machine. But it was her glowing smile and fun conversation that made the time go by so quickly. He never thought he'd be thankful for Birdie meddling in his personal life, but in this case, he was extremely thankful.

The week was flying by. He needed a way to slow it down—to extend his time with Lainey—but he had no idea how to do it. Time just kept slipping away.

It was already Wednesday, and they had plans that evening to get together and make a big sign for the event. Lainey had already sent him a store list of supplies they'd need for the sign. He was a little worried when he saw the list included pink, yellow, and blue glitter. What in the world was she going to do with those? Then again, maybe he didn't want to know.

He finished working early that day. After shopping for supplies, he picked Lainey up after her shift at the furniture store. They headed back to his place. In addition to the glitter, he had a couple of surprises in store for her.

When she stepped into his apartment, she asked, "What smells so good?"

A smile played at the corners of his lips. "I might have made us some dinner. I hope you like spaghetti and meatballs."

She smiled at him. "Most definitely."

Tux ran over to them. His cat totally snubbed him and went directly to Lainey. He let off a loud purr as he rubbed against her legs. Lainey leaned down and picked up the little traitor. As she held Tux, the cat blinked his eyes at Jack, as though to say Lainey liked him better.

Jack moved to the kitchen. "I can't promise that the meatballs will be any good, but I followed my mother's recipe."

Her smile broadened. "I bet they're delicious. Is it ready to eat?"

He nodded. "I finished it before I picked you up. And I might have a surprise for dessert too."

"A surprise? I can't wait." She turned to him. "You really didn't have to go out of your way for me, but I appreciate it."

"It's been a long time since I had someone around to cook for. I just hope my cooking skills aren't too rusty."

"By the smell of things, you did just fine."

He couldn't deny that his chest puffed up ever so slightly at her compliment. He just hoped he'd done his mother's recipe justice.

"Were you able to find everything for the poster?" Her gaze moved to the coffee table where he'd placed the bag of supplies.

"Yes. Including the glitter." It was on the tip of his tongue to inquire about its usage, but he decided it was better to just be surprised.

To Tux's displeasure, Lainey deposited him on the couch and then joined Jack in the kitchen. They washed up, and then he had her take a seat at the little table off the galley kitchen, which was set for two. He'd placed a red rose in a bud vase for the centerpiece. He wasn't sure what color rose to get her. He knew the different colors had different meanings.

But he was no expert on romance and certainly not on the meaning of roses. And so, he picked out the most perfect flower for the most beautiful woman he'd ever known.

The special thing about Lainey was that her beauty wasn't just skin deep. Her beauty started on the inside with her kindness and generosity. It warmed the world around her with her radiant smiles.

"This is beautiful." Lainey's voice drew him from his thoughts. She leaned over to sniff the rose.

"I'm glad you like the table setting because I can't make any promises about the dinner itself."

She turned to him. "I can't wait to try it."

He served up the meal, which included a tossed salad he already had prepared in the fridge and some garlic bread he slid into the oven while he put the dressing on the salad.

To his great relief, the meal went really well. And his mother would be pleased to know he hadn't made a mess of her recipe. In fact, the spaghetti was more than edible. He might actually make it again. That was if he could talk Lainey into dining with him again.

Even though she'd complimented everything about the meal, he'd noticed she was distracted.

Hoping she'd open up to him, he asked, "What's on your mind?"

She shook her head. "You don't want to hear about it."

"Sure I do, or I wouldn't have asked."

She hesitated. "I just can't stop thinking about the photo of the lighthouse and wondering what it means."

"What do you think your mother was hiding from you?"

"I don't know. That's the problem."

He could see the frustration clouding her eyes. "What do you suspect?"

Lainey let out a deep sigh as she leaned back in her chair. She placed her napkin next to her plate. "I think my parents separated right before she got pregnant with me."

"And why do you think she went on the road trip?"

"I think she was confused about the future and was trying to figure out what to do."

"Sounds like someone I know."

Lainey shook her head. "I went on this trip to follow in her footsteps."

"But did you? Really? You already said you weren't sure about returning to your career as an attorney. Aren't you looking for your own answers?"

Her gaze met his and held. "I never thought of it that way. Maybe you're right."

"As for your parents, every couple fights, so I don't think you have anything to worry about."

"I want to believe you, but I can't get past the feeling that there's more to the story of her cross-country trip. And the fact that my father won't discuss any of it with me just makes me even more curious. They were so open about other parts of their pasts. So, why was this period so secretive?"

He reached his arm across the table and covered her hand. He squeezed it. "Or you miss your mother so much that you're desperate to keep her memory fresh in your mind, and this journey was a way for you to do that."

She looked as though she wanted to vehemently deny his summation, but then she appeared to give it some thought. With a shrug, she said, "Maybe."

Together they cleaned up the dishes. He always hated doing the dishes, but having Lainey next to him gave him a new perspective on the chore. All you needed was someone special to help, and it took the mundane out of the task and made it almost fun. *Almost* being the key word because they were still washing dishes. But he'd be willing to do dishes every day with Lainey next to him.

Once the kitchen was set to rights, the leftovers were wrapped and placed in the fridge, and they moved to the living room. Tux was curled up on the end of the couch. When he saw that he had company, he stood up and stretched.

"I think we're disturbing him." Lainey reached over to pet Tux.

The cat let out a loud purr as he rubbed against her hand.

"From the sounds of it, you have nothing to worry about. He likes you," Jack observed. "And he's not the only one."

She turned to him with a smile on her face. "So, if I pet your head will you purr for me?" Her eyes twinkled with amusement.

He stepped closer to her. He placed his hands on her hips. "I don't know. Let's give it a try."

Her smile broadened as she shook her head. "You aren't serious."

"I'm very serious. Go ahead."

She rolled her eyes, but when she raised her hand to him, he drew her into his embrace. "What are you doing?"

"Making it easier for you to pet my head."

Suspicion shone in her eyes now. Still, she reached up and ran her fingers through his hair. He enjoyed her gentle touch. And then he dipped his head and captured her lips with his own. His heart thump-thumped.

Her lips were soft. And when she opened her mouth to him, she tasted sweet like the frothy citrus drink he'd made to go with her dinner.

Lainey pulled back much sooner than he wanted. He was worried she was upset with his playful kiss, but when he looked into her eyes, he didn't see any anger in their golden-brown depths.

She moved out of his embrace. "That was not purring."

"No. It was a lot more fun."

Her cheeks took on a rosy hue. "We...uh, got sidetracked. We better get started on the poster before it gets late."

And then he remembered that he had a surprise for her. "Just one more thing."

"What is it?"

"Close your eyes."

"Jack, if we keep kissing, we'll never get the poster made."

"And that would be a problem?" This time he was perfectly serious.

"Jack..."

"Okay. Okay. This time there will be no kissing." Although, he much preferred the kissing. "Now close your eyes."

Once she had her eyes closed, he went to get her treat. As he approached her, he held the items behind his back. "Are you peeking?"

"Maybe."

"Lainey, no cheating."

With a huff, she said, "Okay. My eyes are closed. What's my surprise?"

"Hold out your hands." When she did as he asked, he placed an item in each hand.

When her eyes opened, she looked at her hands and smiled. "A whoopie pie. My favorite. And sparkles?"

"You have to choose which you want to do next. Eat your dessert? Or make the poster?"

There was no hesitation. "I definitely want the whoopie pie next, but someone fed me a huge delicious meal. So sadly, it's going to have to wait until we get our work done. Are you ready to get glittered?"

He had a feeling his living room was going to sparkle after they got done with whatever Lainey had in mind. And a couple of weeks ago, he'd have had a problem with that, but as long as Lainey was here to help make the mess, he was all in.

Chapter Seventeen

Delayed again.

Thursday afternoon, Jack didn't understand why his boss kept pushing off their meeting. Jack had time to go over his latest proposal—again. The extra time had given him a chance to fine tune it. He didn't think he could make it any better.

It was his biggest and best campaign to date. It was going to be his springboard into asking about a promotion. He'd been employed by the same company since he'd graduated college. He'd worked his way up through the company. He liked it there. He could see his future with the company.

And that was another reason he intended to move to New York City. The higher he moved up in the company, the more hands-on he needed to be. He was all right with that. He worked with a fabulous team. There was even a chance he'd get to stay in contact with Lainey.

He thought about the last couple of evenings they'd spent together. She made him happy. She just had this special quality that had him smiling when he was around her.

Knock. Knock.

Jack's immediate thought was that it was Lainey at the door. She must have finished work at the furniture store a little early. With a smile on his face, he rushed to the door and flung it open. There stood his brother Liam. The smile slipped from his face.

"Obviously, I'm not the person you were expecting." Liam pressed his hands to his waist.

"Sorry. I just thought you might be someone else."

"Would her name happen to be Lainey?"

Jack frowned at his brother. "Yes, it would."

"I see. Are you going to invite me in?"

Jack backed up, opening the door wider. "Sorry. Come in."

Once inside, Liam glanced around. "Hey, nice poster. I guess Birdie roped you into helping with spring fling."

He nodded. "She did."

"I just didn't see you as the glitter type." Liam arched a brow.

Jack glanced down to see glitter reflecting on the front of his shirt. He fondly recalled their evening together. "The glitter was Lainey's idea. She wanted it for the poster. When I went to move it a little bit ago, I must have gotten some of it on me."

Liam smiled and shook his head.

Feeling a bit paranoid, Jack brushed at the front of his shirt. "What? You never saw someone covered with glitter?"

"It's not that. It's the smile you've got on your face when you mentioned Lainey. I guess that accident had a happy ending after all."

"I definitely wouldn't recommend it for a first meet. But she's forgiven me. And we've become friends."

"Friends?" There went the arched brow again.

Jack thought of the kisses they'd shared. The hand holding. The confiding in each other. It was definitely more than he would do with a friend. "Okay. Maybe we're more than friends."

"Way to downplay it. Have you told her about your theory of being more than friends?"

Jack shook his head. He'd been keeping his feelings so close to his vest for so long it wasn't natural for him to reveal them to anyone. But maybe his brother was right—for once. He should go talk to her—really talk to her. Maybe there was a chance he could have a serious relationship again. With Lainey, he felt like anything was possible.

He wanted to go find her right that moment. But his brother didn't seem like he was going anywhere anytime soon. "I doubt you stopped by to discuss my dating life. What did you need?"

"How do you think Lainey feels about kids?"

"Kids? If you're trying to rush along this relationship, you can just stop there."

"Relax, little brother. I just wanted to know if you could watch Tate tomorrow night. I wanted to take

Mel to the Mainland to celebrate her birthday and our engagement."

"Oh, sure. I can watch him." He loved spending time with his nephew.

"Are you sure? I don't want to mess up whatever it is that you have going on with Lainey."

"It'll be fine."

"Okay. I have to get going. I have a few other things to do before our big date. I'll drop Tate off tomorrow around four."

"Sounds good."

Once Liam was gone, Jack tried calling Lainey, but she didn't pick up. She must have a last-minute customer at the furniture store. He would go surprise her.

Maybe they could pick up some tacos for dinner from Katrina's Kantina. And on the way, he would tell her how much she'd come to mean to him. As much as he'd been fighting it, she'd worked her way past all of his defenses. He was falling for her.

She missed him.

Lainey stood behind the checkout counter at Turner Furniture. She'd just completed a sale, and as soon as she thanked the customer, her thoughts had turned back to Jack. She couldn't wait to see him. She'd never been this drawn to a person in her life. And then there were those oh-so-sweet kisses—those toe-curling kisses. If she wasn't careful, she could end up losing her heart during one of those kisses.

Jack was such a great guy. She could really see this relationship lasting, if it wasn't for one glaring problem. She knew about the demise of his employer. When Jack lost his job, he wouldn't be able to move to the city. And where would that leave them?

"Is everything all right?"

She jumped. Pressing a hand to her pounding chest, she turned to Kent. "Sorry. I didn't hear you approach. Um, yes. Everything is fine."

His brows drew together. "You looked like you had something serious on your mind."

Maybe she needed someone else's perspective. "Hypothetically, if you knew something important that would affect someone else's life, would you tell them?"

"You mean like if you knew someone was cheating on their spouse?" When she shrugged and nodded, he said, "If I cared about the party being cheated on, I would tell them."

"Even if it would cost you something important in life like..." Her mind raced as she searched for an example. "Like losing your business."

His brows scrunched up as he tried to make sense of her example. "I don't know how telling the truth to a friend would affect my business."

"I know. It's a stretch. Oh, never mind. I shouldn't have said anything." When she went to walk away, he reached out to her.

When she stopped, his hand fell away. "I don't know what you're dealing with so I'm not sure my answer to that scenario would help you. All I can tell you is that if I truly loved the person, I would do whatever I could to care for them. And I would then deal with the fallout. My family is more important than any business. I can always start a new business, but I can't replace my family."

His words hit home with her. She knew what she needed to do. She checked the time. "Thank you. I think I'll take your advice. Do you mind if I leave a few minutes early?"

"Not at all. Go. I'll lock up... And I hope things work out for your friend."

"Me too."

She grabbed her things and rushed out the door. She had to tell Jack the whole truth—her real name, her father's company and the ultimate loss of his job.

She was in such a hurry she didn't see the man walking toward her. She ran directly into him.

"Oh. I'm sorry." She took a step back and tilted her chin upward. Her mouth gaped. "What are you doing here?"

"Hello, Daughter." Her father stared back at her.

She noticed he didn't bother to answer her question. "How did you find me?"

"It's not hard to have someone track your phone."

He was right, but she didn't think he'd stoop that low. "I can't believe you'd do that."

"And I can't believe you would continue to dig into your mother's past after I asked you to leave it alone."

"I couldn't. There was something Mother wanted to tell me." Emotion roughened her voice as she thought of the last time she'd talked to her mother in the hospital. "At the end... She, uh, said there was something important she had to tell me."

He waved away her words. "It could have been anything. I don't want to discuss this here on the sidewalk."

She didn't care where they had this conversation. She was tired of waiting for the perfect moment for her father to confide in her because there never would be one.

"This is why you've been so distant since your mother died, isn't it?" His gaze searched hers. "How did you find out about Bluestar Island?"

So she was right. The *BS* in her mother's journal stood for this island. She wasn't ready to tell her father about the journal. She was certain if he knew she had it, he'd demand she return it, and she wasn't ready to do that.

She didn't have the answers she was searching for, but she felt as though she were on the verge of figuring out what her mother wanted to tell her before the illness had stolen away her ability to communicate.

"Go back to New York." She turned to walk away.

He reached out, catching her upper arm with his steely grip. She whipped back around. She looked at his hand still holding her arm, and then she glared at him. He quickly relinquished his hold on her.

There was anger and something more in his eyes. Was it fear? If so, what was he afraid she would learn?

This was going to be the perfect evening.

Jack couldn't wait to pick up Lainey. If he played his cards right, maybe they could go for another stroll on the beach. He was certainly looking forward to it.

And tomorrow he could introduce her to Tate. They were going to hit it off. No one could resist his nephew's little laugh. It was contagious. Tate played hard and laughed harder. He would wear himself out in no time. And once he was asleep, Jack would have a chance to kiss Lainey again.

But tonight, beneath the moon and stars, he would tell Lainey how much he cared about her. Something told him it wouldn't come as a huge surprise to her. Then they could talk about the future—their future in New York City.

He didn't think he'd ever be ready to think about the future. Getting through the here and now had been all he was prepared to deal with. But Lainey had opened his mind and his heart. He felt strong enough to take a chance again.

His steps quickened. He couldn't wait to see her. He hoped he didn't miss her at the store. He turned the corner and spotted her standing not far from the store entrance.

There was a tall older man standing near her. Jack didn't recognize the man. It was probably a customer. Lainey had her back to him. But he recognized her hair and her coat.

"Elaine, I didn't come here to fight with you," the man said.

"Then why did you come?"

"To bring you home, where you belong." The man's voice was firm, like he wasn't used to anyone standing up to him. "And I'm not leaving here without you."

Jack's steps slowed. He recognized the man. It was Lance Devereaux. He was one of the richest men in the country. This man, he was Lainey's father?

Jack's mind started to spin with the implications of this discovery. Lainey wasn't just some woman who lost her memory and needed help. She was an heiress to an empire that was built on buying up companies and breaking them down into spare parts to be resold.

There was a distinct silence before Lainey spoke up. "Are you staying here on the island?"

"No. I have a suite in a hotel in Boston. I needed to make sure I have good internet access. You know this couldn't come at a worse time because my focus should be on the business. We've just finalized the acquisition of Sharps Unlimited."

The breath caught in the back of Jack's throat. He couldn't believe what he was hearing. Her father was acquiring his company. It was next on the chopping block. And Lainey knew about this but didn't tell him?

No. This couldn't be right. The Lainey he'd gotten to know wouldn't do that. She wouldn't let him set himself up for a fall. And yet he thought back to the way his boss had been putting him off all week. That wasn't normal. And now he knew why.

All of the work he'd put into the advertising campaign was for naught. The company would soon not exist thanks to Lainey's father.

Jack stepped up to Lainey. There was still a part of him that didn't want to believe any of this. When Lainey caught his image out of the corner of her eyes, she turned to him. He needed her to tell him he'd jumped to the wrong conclusion, but his gut told him he'd jumped to the right conclusion.

Her eyes widened in surprise. "Jack, what are you doing here?"

Apparently he was there to have his trust thrown back in his face and to have his scarred heart shredded. He choked down his assumptions. He owed Lainey the benefit of the doubt.

His gaze searched hers, seeing torment and pain. "Lainey, is it true? Did you know that I was losing my job? That there was going to be a takeover?"

Her eyes shimmered with unshed tears. She nodded.

His heart sank. "Why would you keep this from me? And let me go on about my plans?"

"I'm sorry." She blinked repeatedly. "I wanted to tell you, but I couldn't. I told you I was an attorney. This deal, I worked on it. If I told you about it, I would have lost my law license. I wanted to tell you, but I was barred from telling you what I knew. I'm so sorry."

He felt betrayed by the one person that let him believe it was okay for him to go on living—to start over. It was a sucker punch straight to his chest because he never even suspected it was coming.

He stared into her eyes as they shimmered with unshed tears. "I opened up to you about the most devastating time in my life, and you couldn't even warn me that your father was about to put me out of work."

When she spoke, her voice cracked with emotion. "Jack..."

He waved off her words as he turned on his heel and strode away. There was nothing she could say to fix this. Nothing at all.

He'd been wrong. He couldn't go forward and forge a new life. This was just more penance for his past.

Chapter Eighteen

THUNDER SHOOK THE INN.

Friday morning, Lainey stared out the window at the dark, stormy sky. The wind pushed at the walls of the inn, making it creak and groan under the force.

She'd been awake most of the night. Thinking about everything that had transpired the night before. She'd gone to Jack's apartment right after leaving her father. He either hadn't been home, which she wanted to believe. Or he'd ignored her pounding on the door, begging for him to talk to her.

She had returned to the inn wet and emotionally exhausted. All night her thoughts had ping-ponged between her huge regret with the horrible way Jack learned the truth and her anticipation about speaking with Maude Clemmons. Her father had let his cards show when he'd asked her how she'd learned about Bluestar Island. She was more certain than ever that Maude would be able to help fill in the blanks.

And then there was her father, who was bound to return to the island that day. After he'd witnessed her encounter with Jack, he was even more insistent about not leaving without her. She inwardly groaned. The man was so stubborn.

Now in the morning light, she halted her thoughts. They only succeeded in making her head ache and her stomach nauseous. She didn't know if it was from the stress or the lack of sleep. Perhaps it was a combination of both.

After taking some painkillers, she reached for the phone. She apologized to Kent for not being able to make it to work that day. Kent thanked her for everything she'd done to help him out. He told her with the bad weather, business would be slow that day, so he probably would have sent her home early anyway.

After she showered and dressed, she took one of the inn's covered carts and drove to Maude's house. As she pulled up in front of the house, her phone rang. She pulled it out of her pocket, hoping after some sleep that Jack was ready to speak to her. Instead, the caller ID showed it was her father. She declined the call. She muted her phone before stuffing it back into her pocket.

With the rain pouring down, she rushed to the covered porch. Her empty stomach was twisted up in knots. She lifted her hand and rapped her knuckles on the robin's-egg blue door.

The seconds felt like very long minutes as she waited for the woman to open the door. She was about to knock again when the door opened.

An older woman with gray hair pulled back in a bun stood there. Her brown eyes squinted as she stared at her. Her complexion was ivory. There was something about her that looked familiar, but Lainey was certain they hadn't met before.

"Can I help you?" The woman reached into the pocket of her gray cardigan. She pulled out a pair of red-framed eyeglasses and perched them on her nose.

"My name's Lainey, I mean Elaine." Those were the only words she got out before the woman's face lost all of its color.

The woman gaped as she stared at Lainey as though she'd just seen a ghost.

"Louise?" The woman's voice was barely more than a whisper. "But it can't be you."

Maude took a step back that was more like a stumble. Lainey was afraid the woman would fall over. "Let me help you sit down."

Lainey rushed forward and took her arm. She helped her sit down in a nearby armchair in what appeared to be the living room. Once the woman was seated, Lainey asked, "Can I get you some water?"

Maude shook her head. "You look so much like my Louise."

The woman seemed to be a bit confused. Maybe it was best that Lainey started over at the beginning. "My name is..." She decided to go with her legal name. "My name is Elaine Devereaux."

Maude's mouth gaped wide open. Her gaze searched Lainey's face, as though she were trying to make sure she was real. Lainey didn't think it was possible, but even more color leached from the woman's face.

Glancing around, Lainey noticed the kitchen through an arch. "I'm going to get you some water."

The woman nodded. This would give each of them a chance to gather themselves. It took Lainey a couple of tries to find the right cabinet with the glasses. With a glass full of water, she returned to the living room. She handed it to Maude and then perched on the edge of the couch.

The woman took a drink. When she set aside the water, she asked, "Are you Janice's daughter?"

Lainey felt as though this were the most profound moment of her life. "Yes. She's my mother."

The woman gasped.

Lainey's insides shivered with nerves. "How... How do you know my mother? Are you a friend? A relative?"

Maude shook her head. "You shouldn't be here. You need to ask your mother these questions."

"I can't." She swallowed hard. "She passed away last year."

"Oh, no." Tears immediately spilled onto Maude's pale cheeks. She grabbed a tissue from her pocket and dabbed her cheeks. "I... I didn't know. I'm so sorry."

Emotions rushed up in the back of her throat, blocking off her breath. Tears burned the backs of Lainey's eyes. She blinked repeatedly as she swallowed hard. She couldn't fall apart. She needed to find the truth.

Once she'd subdued her rising emotions, Lainey said, "I have questions, and I'm hoping you can help me learn the truth. I know my mother was keeping something from me. She tried to tell me about an important secret but... She died before she could."

The woman's gaze searched hers. "Did you ask your father?"

Lainey sighed. She thought of lying to the woman and telling her he was supporting her search for the truth, but she couldn't do it. She wasn't a liar.

Lainey wrung her hands. "He won't talk about it. He either changes the subject or pretends he doesn't hear me."

"Maybe he is trying to protect you."

"Protect me from what?"

The woman took another drink of water. Her hand trembled. A little of the water sloshed over the side. "Your mother... She was... She was my niece. After your grandparents died, she came to live with me."

"You're my aunt?" She had family? After hearing all of her life that her mother had no family, it was a lot to take in.

Maude nodded. "I suppose I am."

It wasn't exactly the answer she was expecting. There was a bit of hesitancy in her voice. Maybe Maude didn't want her mother or her. But why? It wasn't like she'd come to the woman wanting anything other than the truth, but maybe the woman was slow to warm to people. Yes, that must be it.

Maude set aside the glass of water and wiped the spilled water from the back of her hand onto her sweater. "The last time I saw your mother, she was having problems getting pregnant. She had tests done and learned she was infertile."

Infertile? But that was impossible. She'd given birth to her. Lainey had seen the picture of her parents at the hospital right after her birth. Her mother had been in a gown in a hospital bed, and her father had been holding her in his arms.

"That can't be right," Lainey said. "My mother gave birth to me."

Maude hesitated and then nodded. "I had a daughter named Louise."

"Louise?"

"Yes. After your mother came to live with us, those two girls were more like sisters than cousins."

Lainey leaned back on the couch. Her mother had this whole other life that she'd never told Lainey anything about. Why would she do something like that? Lainey had always thought they were uniquely close—such good friends. Now she had to wonder if that was true.

"Louise is my middle name." Her breaths came faster. Question after question raced through her mind. What did this all mean?

It felt like there was a band around her lungs, and she couldn't take in enough air. With each tormenting thought, the band tightened, making it harder to breathe. She wasn't her parents' child? She was adopted? *No. No. That can't be right.*

"What... What are you trying to tell me?" Lainey stared at the woman, hoping whatever she said next would make this better. But at this point was that even possible?

"Your mother and my Louise were so close. It was hard on them when your mom went off to college. They both knew that things would never be the same again. Still, they talked on the phone all of the time. So, after your mother married your father, and she couldn't get pregnant, she refused to give up. They ran tests and found out your mother was infertile. She was distraught. She left your father and set off on a journey. I'm not sure what she expected to gain from her trip. I'm not even sure she knew, but eventually, her journey led her home to this island."

Lainey wanted to rush along this story. She wanted to know how she'd come to be, but she knew this wasn't her story. She had to give Maude time to tell the story in her own way. Lainey laced her fingers together to keep from fidgeting, and she waited with bated breath.

"I'm not sure how the rest came about because Louise and your mother spent a lot of time alone at the lighthouse. Some kids grow up and have a treehouse; those two had a lighthouse. Anyway, one day they came to the house and said they had a plan. Louise was going to donate her eggs so your mother could get pregnant."

This was not what Lainey expected to be told. Her mind felt as though it had just exploded with this news. Everything she knew about herself was a lie. And the funny part—not that it was funny as in ha-ha but funny in a strange way—was that she'd grown up thinking she looked like her mother. Now she wondered if she'd only seen what she wanted to see.

Her mom wasn't her mom.

The acknowledgment stabbed at her heart. The pain was immense. Her entire world imploded around her. Her life was a lie.

Moisture dripped onto the back of her hand. She unlaced her fingers to reach up and feel her cheeks were damp with tears.

"I'm so sorry." Maude's voice was filled with emotion.

She didn't feel as though this was the end of the story. If all of this happened, and her mother was so close to Maude and Louise, why hadn't her mother ever mentioned them? She needed to understand. She couldn't keep living with all of the unanswered questions.

"What..." Lainey's voice cracked with emotion. She swallowed hard. "What happened after they told you about their plan?"

Chapter Nineteen

A HEAVY SILENCE ENVELOPED the room.

Lainey struggled to comprehend everything Maude had told her. Her head swam as a war waged within her over whether to believe this woman or not. This couldn't be true.

Maude was quiet for a moment, as though she were lost in her memories. "I told them, both Janice and Louise, that I was vehemently opposed to the idea. I knew it would hurt your mother to hear those words, but I was only trying to protect both of them. I knew something like this would come between the two of them. I told them in the strongest way possible that I wouldn't support this plan." Tears streamed down the woman's face. "I… I thought I was doing the right thing. I loved those two headstrong girls with my whole heart."

Lainey might have trouble believing what the woman was telling her, but she couldn't deny the love she heard ringing out in Maude's voice. If this was all true, how could her mother have kept this from her? She wouldn't have done that.

Maude swiped at the tears on her cheeks, but as soon as they were gone, new tears took their place. "I wanted what was best for both of them. Maybe I handled it all wrong. I don't know." Maude's watery gaze moved to Lainey. "But if you're sitting here, it means they didn't listen to me and went through with the plan anyhow. You ... You look so much like my Louise."

Lainey struggled not to hyperventilate. Maude was telling her that her mother wasn't her mother. Louise, a woman she'd never met, was her mother. And her parents had kept this all from her. Did they really think she'd never learn about it?

Lainey swiped at the tears that kept coming. "Where is Louise? I... I want to meet her."

Maude shook her head. "I'm sorry but you can't. She passed."

Dead? Her biological mother was dead. How can that be? She just learned about her, and yet it's too late. Her parents had stolen her chance to meet the woman who gave Lainey her smile and her brown eyes with the golden flecks. This secret just kept getting worse.

Maude reached into her pockets for more tissues. She offered Lainey one. "One day Louise went to the doctors for a medical procedure, and there was a complication. In a matter of moments, she...she was gone. It was the darkest day of my life. It was so unexpected. And she was my world."

"I'm sorry." Lainey's voice wobbled. Her head ached, and her heart felt as though it were tattered and torn. "My father. Does he know all about this?"

Please, say no. She needed her father to be innocent. She hoped he was as oblivious to all of this as she was. At this moment, she needed him to be the anchor in this storm that was raging all around her. It was threatening to drown her.

"I don't see how your father wouldn't know about the plan." Maude's tone was matter-of-fact. "They would have needed his cooperation for the IVF procedure."

Of course they would. If her mind wasn't so jumbled, battered, and bruised, she would have known the answer to her own question. Her father had kept this from her. It was another sharp stab to her heart.

She turned to Maude with more questions. The words kept tumbling out of her mouth, one after the other. She couldn't understand why her parents had lied to her for her entire life. The people she'd trusted most in her life had kept this gigantic secret from her.

When she finally stopped the barrage of questions, Maude didn't say a word. Lainey noticed that Maude wasn't looking so well. She was still pale, and she looked as though this revelation had taken all of the energy out of her. Lainey's heart went out to the woman. Maude was as stunned by all of this as she was.

"I'm sorry," Lainey said. "I didn't mean to spring all of this on you. I didn't know the answers I was seeking would lead to this."

Maude leaned forward and held out her hand. Lainey hesitated for a moment. She didn't know this woman, and yet she felt an immediate connection to her. She reached out and took the woman's hand in her own. Maude gave her a squeeze.

Maybe Maude could be her anchor in this storm. As soon as the thought came to her, she realized how desperate she felt. She didn't even know Maude. She couldn't be her anchor. Lainey had to be her own anchor.

For now, she had one last question. "My mother kept a photo of the lighthouse in her journal. Do you know why?"

Maude shrugged. "It's hard to tell. I just know the girls loved the place. I was worried about them being out there, but they were teenagers at that point. And nothing I said was going to keep them away from it. The lighthouse has been in my family for generations. I thought I wouldn't have anyone to hand it down to, but now I do."

The lighthouse would be hers. In the grand scheme of things, this revelation was slight compared to learning that her mother wasn't her mother. The one person she'd trusted the most in the world had lied to her, over and over again. How could she have done that?

Maude got to her feet and moved to a chest of drawers. She opened one of the small drawers and retrieved something.

When Maude approached her, Lainey got to her feet. It was time she left. They both had a lot to digest.

Maude walked over to Lainey and held out a key to her. Lainey extended her hand, and Maude placed it on her palm. Lainey's fingers closed around it, the teeth of the key biting into the flesh of her fingers.

"Your mother stayed at the lighthouse the last time she was on the island—the time when they came up with the idea for your conception. I didn't see her after that visit. Sometimes things are said in the heat of the moment that can't be taken back. It's what happened to us. My wish for you is that you never speak out in the heat of the moment. Words can be a powerful weapon. Listen to an old woman who has to live with her regrets. Choose your words wisely."

"I... I will." She had a feeling Maude was referring to Lainey's eventual confrontation with her father.

"And be very careful if you go to the lighthouse. It hasn't been maintained in years. It could be dangerous."

"I'll be careful." Lainey's gaze searched Maude's. She'd lied. She had another question. "What does this make us?"

Maude's eyes filled with fresh tears. Lainey didn't know if they were happy or sad ones. Perhaps they were a bit of both.

"You, my dear, are my precious granddaughter."

Lainey's mouth opened, but there was a complete disconnect between her mind and her mouth. There was a part of her that wanted to rush to the woman and throw her arms around her. She'd never had a grandmother before.

And yet there was another part of her that struggled to come to grips with learning that everything she thought she knew about herself was a lie. Her mother was not her mother. Her mother was what? Her second cousin? Or first cousin once removed? It was just too much.

Lainey felt weighted down under all these revelations. She felt utterly sick to her stomach. She couldn't stop asking questions, and her mind just couldn't absorb anymore. She pressed a hand to her stomach. She was going to be sick. The only answer was to leave.

She looked at Maude. "I... I have to go."

Lainey turned and rushed out the door. She drove the cart back to the inn. In that moment, she regretted her stubbornness to find the truth. She wished she'd never found that journal. She wished her mother had taken all of her truth to the grave with her.

Because Lainey had never felt this alone in her life—not even at her mother's funeral. She felt adrift. She was not her mother's daughter. The thought circled in her mind at a dizzying pace. This couldn't be so, and yet it was.

Why hadn't her father told her? He knew she had questions. He knew how stubborn she could be. He knew she wouldn't stop until she uncovered the truth. And now her world had blown up. Nothing would be the same again.

As she approached the inn, she spotted a man pacing back and forth across the large covered porch. She slowed her bike to a stop. She knew that dark head of hair and those broad shoulders as well as that charcoal gray suit that fit the man so well. It was her father.

Her first instinct was to march right up to him and vent all of her anger at him. It would come roaring out of her like an enraged lioness. His silence had ended up slicing her heart in the worst way. She didn't know that she would ever forgive him.

In the back of her mind was the voice of Maude warning her to choose her words wisely. She couldn't do that right now. Her emotions were raw and jagged. Tears streamed down her face.

She wanted to hurt her father as badly as he had hurt her. It would be too easy to march right up to him and tell him how much she hated him. She knew that verbal barb would strike right at his heart. The only problem was that she didn't hate him. She hated what he did, but she didn't hate him. And yet she couldn't just forgive him. It wasn't going to happen.

She needed time to figure out all she was feeling. She didn't want to make this worse, but she didn't know how it could become any more devastating.

Her father hadn't seen her yet, so she changed directions. She wasn't ready to confront him yet.

She found herself heading toward Jack's place. She really needed him now. He would listen to her. He really heard her words. He didn't push his ideas on her, but if she asked for his opinion, he would give it.

And she missed him so much. She could really use one of his bear hugs. Because when she was in his arms, the rest of the world faded away.

Then reality came crashing in on her. He was angry with her. He wasn't taking her calls. Well, too bad. She was going to his place, and they would work things out.

When she got there, she knocked on his door. He didn't answer.

She knocked again. "Jack, I'm not leaving until you open this door."

"Jack isn't home."

Lainey turned her head to see an older woman with short brown hair and a warm smile. "Do you know where he went?"

The woman shook her head. "He left a while ago and seemed to be in a hurry."

"Thanks."

She returned to the cart. She had nowhere to go. And then she realized there was one place she could go where no one would bother her. And so with the thick dark clouds hanging overhead, she started off for the lighthouse.

The road was quiet with only a couple of carts that passed her. She got a couple of strange looks from the passersby because this was not the sort of day for sightseeing. The wind was blowing as dark clouds scudded across the sky.

None of it mattered to Lainey. The sky could open wide and dump rain on her, and it wouldn't stop her.

As though Mother Nature intended to test her resolve, a big fat raindrop pinged against the cart's roof. Another followed it, and then the sky really did open up, and she was in the middle of a downpour.

She didn't care. She squinted to see through the raindrops. When she reached the end of the road, she didn't let the rain stop her. She set off through the overgrown path. It was the only way to the lighthouse. She just hoped she didn't lose her way, because in the dark shadows of the storm, none of it looked familiar.

In her rush to get to the lighthouse, her foot caught on a tree root. She tried to catch her balance, but with all of the rain, the ground was muddy, and her other foot slipped. Down she went.

Her hands and knees hit the ground. Wet mud smushed between her fingers. Just perfect. She struggled to her feet. It wasn't easy. The mud was slick. Once she had her balance, she wiped her hands off on the clean part of her jeans. Could this day get any worse?

She kept going. All the while she replayed her conversation with Maude. When she made it to the beach, her tennis shoes were squashy with rain water. It didn't matter. She was almost at the lighthouse.

As lightning lit up the sky, her chest ached. She couldn't get past her mother not being her mother. She loved her mother so deeply. How could she have done this to her? Why did she do it?

As the thunder shook the ground, her thoughts turned to her father. She had a feeling he was on Bluestar Island, hoping to do some damage control. Did he really think he could treat her like one of his business deals that had gone wrong? There was no damage control that was going to fix any of this.

At last she made it to the lighthouse. When she reached for the key in her pocket, her hands were shaking. Was it from the wind and rain chilling her skin? Or from the shock of everything she'd learned? She realized she didn't care. She just had to get the key in the lock. It took a couple of tries.

She swung the door open and stepped inside. Alone at last, she opened her mouth to let out her pent-up emotions. Pain, betrayal, confusion mingled together, and instead of words, everything came out in a loud cry of agony.

Her scream echoed through the tall lighthouse. It went on and on; she didn't think she'd ever get out all of the agony.

When she couldn't cry out any longer, she fell to her knees in the shadows. Tears streamed down her cheeks, falling to the dirty wooden floor. She cried for the mother that was no longer in her life. She cried for the mother she never knew. She cried for the father that she'd always looked up to. She cried for the man that she'd fallen in love with that wouldn't even speak to her anymore. And she cried for herself because she didn't know who she was any longer.

Chapter Twenty

How could she have not told him the truth?

Jack felt as though he'd lost someone very special to him. He was angry at Lainey for keeping her real identity from him. She was the heir to LMD Inc. She was a part of the company that had stolen away the job he'd had for so many years. His co-workers that he valued were stripped away. His plans for the future were upended.

He never should have let his guard down with her. He should have known it was all too easy. He wondered what else she'd lied about by omission. If he hadn't stumbled upon the truth, he wondered if she ever would have told him.

Knock. Knock.

If it was Lainey, she was wasting her time. He had nothing to say to her—at least nothing she would want to hear. She should have gotten the message when he'd let her numerous phone calls go to voicemail. He didn't want to hear her excuses for keeping the truth from him.

He should just let her stand there and knock until she got bored and moved on. Then again, she might take it as an invitation to come back another time. He didn't want that. He wanted this over, once and for all.

He strode over to the door and swung it open. "I don't want to talk to you."

"Whoa." Grant, his oldest brother, stood there with his eyes wide open while confusion was written all over his face. "What did I do to you?"

"Nothing." Jack's answer was clipped. Lainey had him so riled up he was acting out of character. He blew out a breath.

"Can I come in?"

Jack opened the door wider and walked away. This was not a good time for a visit, but Grant wasn't around very often. Grant was a doctor at one of the big hospitals in Boston. He didn't get a lot of time off, so his visits were rare.

"I came to the island for Spring Fling." Grant moved toward the couch and proceeded to pet Tux. "Seems I arrived at the right time or maybe the wrong time. What's bothering you? And who don't you want to speak to?"

Jack didn't want to get into any of this with his brother. Jack was used to keeping his feelings tucked deep down inside. It was what he'd done throughout his marriage and the loss of the baby. *And look where that got you*—a voice in the back of his mind taunted.

Maybe his brother could give him some clarity that he was unable to achieve on his own. After they took a seat, Jack said, "There was an accident…"

Jack went on to tell Grant about how he'd first met Lainey. He told him about how they'd grown closer. Along the way he revealed about the baby he and Nora had lost.

Grant's gaze shone with sympathy. "Jack, I'm so sorry. Why didn't you tell anyone about the baby? We would have been there for you."

Jack rubbed his stiff neck muscles. "I couldn't, because I blamed myself for the accident."

"But it wasn't your fault."

Jack went to argue with his brother but bit back his words. He was never going to convince his brother it was his fault nor would his brother convince him it wasn't his fault.

"I just don't understand how Lainey could keep the news about my job from me. I thought we trusted each other. This morning, I got the formal notification that I'd been let go."

"Jack..." Grant raked his fingers through his hair. "I don't know what to say. But I know you won't have a problem getting another job."

"I don't know about that. I have to start all over. I don't even have a current resume." Jack couldn't sit still. He got up and paced between the living room and the kitchen.

"I think I know the real problem," Grant said.

"The real problem is that I lost my job, and the woman I trusted lied to me by omission."

"I think there's something more troubling you."

Jack remembered how his big brother used to be a know-it-all when they were kids. He wasn't in the mood for a lecture. "Don't, Grant."

As though Jack hadn't said anything, Grant uttered, "You're in love with her."

"I am not." The answer came out too quickly.

"Yes, you are, but you're fighting it. Why?"

"I already told you what she did. Isn't that reason enough to keep her out of my life."

"Or are you using this to push her away? Are you still punishing yourself for the marriage that fell apart and the baby you lost?" When Jack didn't respond, Grant went on. "Sadly, miscarriages are more common than you would think. And they can happen for any number of reasons. Is continuing to punish yourself the right way to honor your child? Do you really think your son or daughter would want you to be miserable the rest of your life?"

Jack turned on his brother to argue with him. He opened his mouth, but the words clogged the back of his throat. He hated when his big brother made a good point. This wasn't what his child would have wanted for him.

"I can see that you actually heard me for the first time. Why don't you go find Lainey and talk things out? From what you said, it doesn't sound like she intentionally set out to hurt you. Maybe you should hear her out."

He looked at his brother. "When did you get so smart?"

Grant smiled at him. "I am a doctor, remember?"

"I hate to chat and run, but there's food in the fridge. Help yourself. I'll see you later."

Just then a flash of lightning filled the windows. It was dark as night out even though it was only two in the afternoon. Another round of storms was supposed to move through the area. Thunder followed the lightning and rattled the windows.

Grant nodded toward the window. "Are you sure you want to go out in that? Maybe you should wait a while."

He shook his head. He'd already put Lainey off long enough. "I have to go to her." He hesitated. "I'm supposed to watch Tate this evening. If I don't make it back in time, can you take care of him?"

"I'd love to spend some time with Tate. I'll call Liam and work something out. Now go." Grant continued to pet Tux. "I'll let myself out."

Jack didn't even hesitate as he grabbed a raincoat and headed out the door. She should still be at the furniture store. Today was supposed to be her last day working there.

He drove his cart to the store. He parked near the door and rushed inside. His gaze darted around the showroom. Where was Kent? And then he spotted him through the window of the office.

He strode back there, stopping in the doorway. "Do you know where Lainey is?"

Kent glanced up from his computer. "I don't know. She called off this morning and said she wasn't feeling well."

Jack had a feeling he knew what was bothering her—the way things had ended between them.

He continued to prod his brother for information. "She didn't say what she was going to do?"

Kent shook his head. "What's this all about? Are you two fighting?"

"I just need to find her."

"Well, I'd start at the inn. She's probably still there. I told her with the bad weather that business would be slow, so it was no big deal for her to take the day off."

"Thanks." Jack turned and rushed for the door.

On his way out, he reached for his phone. He dialed her number. It went directly to voicemail. "Lainey, it's me. I've been trying to find you. We need to talk. Call me when you get this message."

The rain had switched to a light shower. Jack jumped into his cart and turned toward the inn. He didn't know what he was going to say to her when he saw her. His thoughts hadn't gotten that far. Normally, he planned ahead for all of his meetings but this was different. For once in his life, he was going to have to wing it. No plan. No rehearsed words.

He pulled to a stop in the inn's parking lot. He rushed up the walk, crossed the porch, and swung the front door wide open.

He headed straight for the front desk. His sister was standing there. "Josie, is Lainey in her room?"

Josie shook her head. "She left this morning in one of the carts, and I haven't seen her since." She nodded to a man sitting in the lobby reading his phone. "Her father is looking for her too."

Anger pumped through Jack's veins as he looked at the man who had taken work away from not only him but his co-workers. He had a lot he wanted to say to the man, but his priority was reaching Lainey.

Where would she ride to on the island? It wasn't like she had friends on the island. He thought of the places they'd visited together. They'd gone to various restaurants. There was the boulder on the beach. She wouldn't be in any of those places. She was upset. She would go someplace private.

And then it came to him. She'd gone to the lighthouse. She seemed really captivated by the lighthouse. But in this weather, would she really go all the way out there?

He turned back to his sister. "If Lainey returns, call me."

"What do you want with my daughter?" The deep voice came from behind him.

Jack inwardly groaned before he turned to the man. "If you must know, I care about your daughter, and I need to find her."

The man's gaze narrowed as he focused on Jack like he was the enemy. "You didn't sound like you cared about her when you confronted her yesterday."

"I don't have time for this." Jack moved past the man.

"If you're going to find my daughter, I'm going with you."

Those words brought Jack up short. He turned around. "Everything was fine with Lainey until you showed up. She was happy. We were happy. Now she's taken off. Did you ever think that she's avoiding you?" Jack noticed that the man for once had nothing to say. "You need to stay here. I'll find Lainey, and then she can choose whether to see you or not."

Jack didn't give the man time to respond. He turned and took long, quick strides outside. He had to find Lainey. The thought she'd be at the dilapidated lighthouse in this weather worried him.

She'd cried her heart out.

Lainey didn't think she had any tears left to shed. Her chest ached. Her heart felt as though it were in a million pieces.

Her teeth chattered. She was so cold as she lay on the floor in the fetal position. Her clothes were soaked and clinging to her body. Goosebumps raced over her limbs.

She dragged herself upright. She'd forgotten how cool it could get in the springtime. And there was absolutely no heat in the lighthouse. She got to her feet and moved to the wall. She searched and found a light switch near the door. She flicked it, but no lights came on. She had a feeling the power had been turned off long ago.

The wind blew so hard the windows rattled. She braced herself for them to blow out, but thankfully, they didn't. As the rain pelted the glass, she reached for her phone and turned on the flashlight app. It appeared this floor of the lighthouse contained the living area. There was a living room and kitchen. She slowly made her way around the floor.

She opened every drawer and every door. She didn't know what she was searching for. It wasn't like her mother would have left her a letter here. Her mother—both of her mothers—hadn't known their lives were about to end. Neither had a chance to make things right, to say whatever was weighing on their hearts.

And yet Lainey kept searching. It took her a bit to finish checking the main floor. She didn't find anything that was a link to her mother... Her mothers. She didn't know if she'd ever get used to saying mothers.

She turned, and her gaze settled on the wooden stairs that curved their way up the outside wall. She craned her neck upward at the exposed beams overhead.

She wondered what was up there. She moved to the steps. As her foot touched the first step, it let out a loud creak. She tightened her hold on the rustic handrail on the outside of the steps. With every step, the stairs shook and groaned.

All of the sudden, there was something in her face. She jumped, clutching the handrail to keep her from tumbling down the steps. She reached for her face and swiped aside a large cobweb. A shiver of revulsion rippled through her. She hated spiders.

She moved slowly and gingerly up one step at a time. The stairs were probably fine. She was just a little nervous with the storm. The bright lightning felt so close, like it was going to strike the lighthouse. The thunder rattled the entire structure. It had her on edge.

When she made it to the second floor, she flashed the beam from her phone around the room. There were two twin beds with a desk between them. On the far wall was a couch and two armchairs. At one point this place must have been quite cozy.

She moved to the window and looked outside. As lightning streaked across the sky, she could see the massive waves pounding on the wall of rocks at the base of the lighthouse. When was this storm ever going to end? She never expected it to get this bad.

She turned her attention back to the room. How could this be her mother's favorite place to spend time, and yet there didn't appear to be any of her belongings?

Lainey made her way across the floor to the desk. She saw a photograph of her mother. She reached for it. She pulled out the push pin, but the photo slipped from her hold. It slipped down between the wall and the desk.

The last thing she wanted to do was crawl under that desk and run into another sticky, creepy cobweb. And yet her desire to retrieve the photo outweighed her arachnophobia.

She pulled out the chair and just as she suspected there were cobwebs. She gritted her teeth and stuck her hand in there. As the cobwebs brushed over her hand, a shiver of revulsion raced over her skin. Her fingers grasped the photo, and she yanked it out.

She leaned back against the bed and held the light on the photo. It was a picture of her mother when she was young, most likely a teenager. She wasn't alone. There was a young woman next to her. They were both smiling, as though they didn't have a care in the world.

Lainey lifted the photo closer to her face. She stared at the other woman. She was certain it was Louise. Now she understood why Maude had thought she was seeing a ghost. The woman looked a lot like Lainey. She didn't know how she felt about that.

Since the shock had worn off, she felt numb. Or maybe she was just emotionally exhausted. Her mind was still trying to come to terms with everything she'd learned.

She placed the photo on the dusty top of the desk. She was taking it with her.

When she went to dust off the wooden desk chair before sitting down, she realized what a ridiculous waste of time that would be. She was soaked and had mud all over her. What would a little, um...a lot of dust matter at this point. She sat down and pulled out drawer after drawer, searching through each and every scrap of paper.

In the bottom drawer, she found some old teen magazines. They were very old—older than her. They must have belonged to her mother or Louise. She kept digging to the bottom, where she found a letter. The return address was her home in Manhattan. It was addressed to Louise.

Lainey turned the envelope over and found it was already open. She pulled out a yellowed piece of paper. She unfolded it and began to read.

Louise,

Thank you! Those two words aren't enough to express the gratitude I have for your generosity. In my heart, you are the sister I never had.

The procedure worked and I'm now twelve weeks pregnant. This is a dream come true—a dream I thought was out of my grasp. If there is ever anything I can do for you, just ask myself or Lane. We are both forever in your debt.

And I promise not to tell Aunt Maude about the baby. I know she's opposed to what we've done. It makes me sad. I miss her so much and would love to share this precious time in my life with her, but I will respect her decision to want nothing to do with it. And I don't want to come between you and your mother.

You are the bestest cousin ever! And I love you. Come to New York soon.

I miss you,
Janice

A pent-up breath escaped her lungs. It was all right there in the letter, confirmation of everything Maude had told her. Lainey swiped the tears from her eyes as she read the letter again.

She had two mothers. Two. And neither was around to answer any of her questions. She'd never felt so alone in her life.

Chapter Twenty-One

THE STORM RAGED.

Jack couldn't remember the last time they'd gotten such a bad storm. But he wouldn't be deterred. If Lainey was out at the lighthouse in this bad weather, he was worried about her.

The fierce wind pushed against Jack's cart, rocking it from side to side. No one was out on the road. He couldn't blame them. He'd much rather be snug at home with Lainey by his side.

Now that he'd had a chance to calm down, he understood why she hadn't told him about his business being taken over. He didn't like it, but he got it.

He reached the end of the road where the path to the lighthouse began. There was an abandoned cart. Lainey was out here.

It took him a while to make it through the overgrowth. The ground was soaked. The mud was slick. He'd almost fallen a couple of times.

He ran a hand through his wet hair. Why would she have come out here in this weather? Liking the lighthouse was one thing, but needing to see it during a raging storm was quite another. And now, as he heard the waves crash upon the shore, he worried she was in trouble.

He made his way across the beach. His raincoat wasn't much help in the wind. Even his shoes were now soaked. And he was cold. Between the rain and the constant wind, he didn't think he'd ever get warm again.

He shielded his eyes and glanced up at the lighthouse. She had to be in there, safe from the storm. But the whole place was so dark. And then he saw a flicker of light in one of the windows. Was that her?

He lowered his head and continued trekking over the wet sand. He had questions, like how did she get inside the lighthouse. As far as he knew, the place had been locked up tight.

At last, he made it to the foot of the lighthouse. The waves were crashing against the boulders that created a wall leading up to the lighthouse. The spray from those waves hit him. The salty water tracked down his face.

He gripped the handrail that lined the steps leading up to the door. Every couple of steps he had to pause as a hefty gust of wind threatened to knock him off the steps and onto the jagged rocks below.

At last, he reached the door. His thumb pressed down on the latch, and to his relief, it released. The wind caught the door and swung it out of his grasp. He stepped inside and had to wait until the gust let up, and then he wrestled the door closed.

He wiped the rain from his face and then squinted into the darkness. He reached out to the wall next to the door and found a light switch. He flicked it, but nothing happened. He wasn't surprised, since the lighthouse had been pretty much abandoned for most of his lifetime.

"Lainey, are you here?" He moved farther into the big room.

His knee hit the end of some sort of little table. He bit back a yelp of pain.

He called out louder this time. "Lainey."

A moment passed, and then she responded. "Jack, is that you?"

"Yes. Where are you?"

"Up here."

He lifted his head but couldn't make out anything in the darkness. He turned on the flashlight app on his phone. He moved it around until he found a rustic set of steps.

He headed toward them. He was so anxious to see Lainey again. And then his phone died. He ran into a chair near the bottom of the steps.

"Are you okay?" Lainey called out.

"Yeah. Just ran into a chair." He stepped on the first stair.

The creak of wood got lost in the howl of the wind. He took hold of the railing and proceeded up the steps. His focus was on what he wanted to say first to Lainey. He was only a few steps from the top. Maybe he should kiss her...

Crack!

The next thing Jack knew, the steps dropped out from beneath him. He was free falling. He reached out but grasped nothing but air.

He was here.

What did it mean?

When Lainey heard him on the steps, she moved to greet him. She had so much to tell him. But then she recalled how angry and hurt he had been when he'd learned the truth about who she was and her father's company.

Her eagerness to see him dimmed. Maybe he was here to yell at her—to tell her how horrible she was to keep news of his company's demise from him. She couldn't deal with that tonight.

Crack!

The floor shook. For a moment she thought the entire lighthouse was collapsing.

She froze in fear. There was a loud crash. And then it all stopped.

The only sound was that of the wind and rain. She rushed over to where the steps had been just a moment ago. She shined her light and found the entire staircase was gone.

Without any railing to hold her back from falling, she hesitated to get too close to the edge. If the stairs collapsed, what were the chances that the entire floor would give way?

"Jack?" There wasn't a sound from him. Her heart pounded. He had to be okay. "Jack, please say something."

She strained to hear over the noise of the storm. She still couldn't hear anything.

Scared that something serious was wrong with him, she got down on her hands and knees. No longer concerned about the spiders or other creepy crawlies, she crawled over to the opening in the floor. She flashed the light down below, but her light wasn't very strong, and there was so much debris. *Oh no.*

"Jack, say something. Please answer me."

There was a cough. Followed by another cough. She had to get to him. She thought of jumping, but it looked so far down. And there was splintered wood all over the floor.

She looked around for something to help her down. At last, she settled on tying some blankets together. She'd seen it on television. They made it look so simple. Surely it would work for her too.

"Don't worry, Jack. I'm coming."

She stripped the bed closest to her. She tied together the blankets and sheet. Then she needed something strong to anchor them too—something that would hold her weight. She chose one of the upright beams that held up the ceiling.

She carefully moved to the edge again. She dangled her legs over the edge. She gave the crudely made rope a hard tug. The beam held its own.

With a death grip on the blanket, she heaved herself over the edge. They made this look so easy on television. But there was nothing easy about it. Her arms weren't strong enough to allow her the ability to lower herself hand over hand.

When she attempted it, her arm gave out, and she landed on the floor with an *oomph*. Her backside was a bit sore, but there were no serious injuries.

She scrambled to her feet. She moved to Jack's side. There were hunks of wood around him and on him.

"Jack?" She started to move the small pieces of wood.

He coughed some more. "I... I'm okay."

"You don't look okay."

"I...had the breath knocked out of me."

She got all except one piece of wood off of him. The last piece was huge. It was a large support for the stairs. The long hunk of wood lay diagonal over his legs.

She bent over, wrapped her arms around it, and attempted to lift it. She couldn't budge the piece of lumber. It had to weigh a hundred pounds or more. This was it. She was going to stop with the excuses and go to the gym regularly.

Jack coughed some more. She didn't like the sound of it. It was possible he had internal injuries.

She tried again. This time her fingertips felt something damp. She stopped and reached for her phone. The light showed it was blood. It was coming from his leg.

"I'm calling nine one one."

"No. We don't need them." He started to sit up. "I'm fine."

She dialed the number. "You're far from fine."

"Nine one one. What's your emergency?"

"I need help. We need help. Jack is pinned."

"What is your name?"

Lainey answered the operator's questions. All the while, Jack struggled to get up, but he couldn't move the big hunk of wood either.

"The ambulance has been dispatched to another scene. I will reroute them to your location as soon as possible."

"Please, hurry. I don't know how serious the injury to his leg is."

And then her phone died. Lainey groaned. She'd used the flashlight app so much it had drained the phone's battery.

In the meantime, she grabbed a cushion from the couch. "Here. Let me put this under your head."

"I want to sit up." He struggled to lift himself onto his elbows.

She placed a firm hand on his shoulder. "Stop."

"Why?"

"Because you fell a long way. We don't know what's wrong with you. Just lay back and rest. There's nothing you can do anyway. We have to wait for help."

"Where are they?"

"I don't know. The operator didn't say."

Once she got the cushion positioned under his head, she noticed his teeth were chattering. She didn't know if it was from his wet clothes or if he was going into shock.

She rushed over to the couch and grabbed an old quilt from the back of the couch. She chose to ignore the cloud of dust that enveloped her when she moved it. She sneezed. And sneezed. And sneezed.

"What are you doing?" Jack called out.

"I'll be right there." When she stopped sneezing, she made her way over to him. She draped the quilt over him. "Is that better?"

"It'd be a lot better if I had a slice of pizza and the game on the television."

She didn't know what to make of his teasing tone in this serious moment. She decided to play along.

"I see how it is." She exaggerated her voice. "I'm not good enough to entertain you. You would rather watch sports."

"And pet my cat. Tux is great company. He never talks during the game."

She huffed. "That will teach me to be nice to you."

"You know after yesterday, I never thought we would be like this again." He held his hand out to her.

She remembered the angry words he'd thrown at her. They'd hurt as well as his belief that she'd set out to hurt him on purpose. But she understood his initial response.

How could she stay upset with him when she understood what it was to be lied to and have the rug pulled out from under her? If anyone could understand what he'd felt, it was her.

She reached out and took his hand in hers. Their fingers laced together.

"I'm sorry," she said.

"It's not your fault. This place is old and needs renovations."

"No. Not the accident, though I do feel horrible about it. I'm talking about what happened with your job. I would have told you if I could. I was blocked because the information was privileged. You know I'm an attorney, even though I'm not working at the moment. And if I had told you I could have been brought up in front of the bar and lost my license."

Jack was quiet for a moment. "I'm not going to lie. I was totally blindsided when I heard you and your father. It hurt to know that you were keeping this from me. It made me wonder what else you're keeping from me."

"Nothing." She was quick to reply. "I swear."

He was quiet for a moment. When he pulled his hand from hers, her heart sank. He didn't believe her.

Then she noticed that he was trying to move. "What's wrong?"

"It's my leg." He struggled again without success.

"I'll try again to move the wood." When she went to move it, he reached out to her.

"Leave it. They will be here soon. And we were having an important conversation." He laced his fingers with hers once more. "I understand why you did what you did."

"You do? I'm so sorry I hurt you. That was not my intention. I never thought I'd be in that position."

"You were stuck in an impossible position. I get that. Let's move past it."

She couldn't believe her ears. This was too good to be true. She was certain it was just the shock from his accident. Once he was feeling better, she was certain he would change his mind. But she didn't want to do anything to upset him while he was injured.

"So why in the world did you come out here in the middle of a storm?" His voice drew her from her thoughts. "I mean I know you like this place. It was written all over your face when we visited. But it would have been here when the storm passed over."

"I..." She struggled to figure out where to start her story. "I went to see Maude Clemmons, who owns this lighthouse. And I learned she's my grandmother."

"What?"

She could tell her words had gained his full attention. She hoped it would distract him from the pain in his leg. She proceeded to tell him everything she'd learned from Maude.

"I feel like I lost my mother all over again." The pain was still so fresh and raw. She thought she didn't have any tears left, and yet some rolled down her cheeks. "I... I don't understand how she could have kept this all from me. I thought we were so close."

Jack squeezed her hand. "I don't think you lost your mother."

"It feels like it. It feels like my whole life was a lie."

"Perhaps instead of losing a mother, you gained one."

It sounded good, but her mind was struggling to absorb it. "Maybe. I don't know. But when I went back to the inn and found my father waiting for me, I just couldn't face him. And that's how I ended up here. Maude gave me the key to the place."

"I think before you spend any more time here, we need to get someone out here to do some repairs."

"I think you're right."

Just then the door swung open, and a gust of wind rushed past them. Beams from flashlights moved over the room.

"We're over here," Lainey said. Then she turned to Jack. "You're going to be all right."

She had to believe that. Once they moved the wooden beam, Jack would be all right. She leaned over to him and went to press her lips to his cheek. but he turned his head, catching her lips with his own.

Her heart fluttered in her chest. With her lips pressed to his, she felt as though anything was possible. She longed for him to feel the same way about her when this traumatic event was over. *Please let it be so.*

Chapter Twenty-Two

It hurt. A lot.

Jack didn't want to let on to Lainey just how badly his leg hurt. He knew it wasn't good, but he didn't want to worry her any more than she already was.

"Hey." Owen, his youngest brother, moved to his side. "What are you doing all the way out here during this crazy storm?"

"Trust me," he said softly, "it wasn't my idea."

"What are you talking about?" Owen, being trained with first aid, worked to stabilize him.

"It's nothing I can get into." His gaze searched through the beams of light to see Lainey. Someone had draped a yellow blanket over her shoulders. "Hey, what took you guys so long?"

"We were on a call. Horace Blackwell was trying to help the Wilsons, whose house was taking on water. He collapsed."

"Is he all right? Did you get there in time?"

"No."

The knowledge weighed heavy on him. Horace had worked so hard to turn his life around. He was just settling in with the community, and he ran out of time. He felt so bad for the guy. Sometimes life wasn't fair.

Jack didn't want that to happen to him. He didn't want to turn into a miserable loner. He had loved his baby, but punishing himself wasn't going to bring his child back—no matter how much he wished that were possible.

He would hold the memory of his baby tightly in his heart, but Lainey had helped him realize there was more room in his heart, if he just took the chance. And he wanted to take that chance with her.

The only problem was now that he didn't have a job, relocating to New York was impossible. And he knew Lainey couldn't stay on Bluestar Island forever. Her life was in the city. He couldn't ask her to sacrifice everything in her life for him. That wouldn't be fair. And it wouldn't work.

So, where did that leave them? With a long-distance relationship? The idea didn't appeal to him.

He noticed someone speaking to Lainey, but in the shadows, he couldn't make out their face.

"Hey, who is that talking to Lainey?"

Owen finished checking his blood pressure and glanced over his shoulder. "I can't really see, but it might be her father. Once he learned we were coming here, he insisted on coming with us."

Jack was shocked her father would ruin his designer suit and expensive dress shoes in order to trek out here during a storm. Perhaps there was more to the man than being a corporate raider.

Perhaps beneath it all, he had a heart. He hoped so for Lainey's sake.

He just has to be all right.

Lainey refused to take her gaze off of Jack. She wanted to be by his side, but there was no room for her. The emergency workers converged around him, preparing to lift the heavy beam off his legs.

She blamed herself for Jack getting injured. She shouldn't have come out here in the storm, and then he wouldn't have followed her. He wouldn't have been on those rickety steps.

He just has to be all right.

She kept repeating the phrase in her head, as though if she said it enough times, it would be true.

"Elaine, we should go back to the inn." Her father's voice reminded her he was still standing there.

"I'm not leaving without Jack." She didn't take her gaze off the man she loved.

She refused to let herself get too excited about what was said between them. Sure, he'd said he forgave her for not telling him the truth about his job being dissolved, but he was going into shock. When he was rescued and feeling better, he could very well come to his senses and tell her he never wanted to see her again.

"Elaine, will you at least look at me?" Her father's voice was laced with exhaustion.

With a group of firefighters blocking her view of Jack, she glared at her father. "What are you doing here?" A tsunami of emotions laced her harsh words. "This is all your fault."

His eyes widened as his dark brows drew together. "My fault?"

It was one of the few times in her life that she'd caught her father off-guard. Pain and anguish churned inside of her. "Yes. If you hadn't lied to me my whole life—if you hadn't let me learn the truth from someone else—Jack wouldn't be lying over there injured and trapped. Just… Just go away. I…"

She caught herself before she uttered the words: *I never want to see you again*. They hovered on the tip of her tongue. They'd be so easy to utter. And yet she knew the damage they'd cause.

She turned away. Somewhere in her heart, buried beneath the agony of deceit and grief, was a tiny flicker of love for the man who had once been at the center of her life. Her father wasn't perfect—even less perfect now—but he'd never walked away from her or her mother. And that deserved some sort of respect, even if he hadn't paid her the same in return.

She sensed him still standing there. She turned, and this time she took in his disheveled appearance. He was soaked from head to foot, like everyone in the room. His short gray hair was flattened to his head, thanks to the rain.

His black overcoat didn't appear to be up for the challenge of a storm or trekking through the foliage. The arm of his coat had a cut and a layer of mud. She didn't think his designer suit and shoes had fared any better.

She was surprised her father would put himself through all of this. Usually he was the one to stay safely behind his desk at the office, while he had his employees deal with the messy situations. He must have sensed she'd learned the truth, and now he'd come to do damage control. Well, too little, too late.

"Elaine, I'm sorry." His voice was ragged with emotion and so soft she wasn't sure she'd heard him correctly.

"For what?" She needed to know exactly what he was apologizing for. The truth he'd kept from her or the peril Jack was now in?

He raked a hand through his wet hair. "For all of it. For not telling you the truth. You have no idea how many long nights your mother and I tried to decide what was best for you."

"What was best was for me to know the truth—that my mother..." Her voice cracked with emotion. She swallowed hard. "That she's not my...not my mother." Her final words came out as a whisper. It was so hard to speak those words—to vocalize them was to give them credence, and she hated it—hated this whole situation.

"But she is your mother. She will always be your mother. She gave birth to you. She cared for you when you were sick. She loved you with her whole heart. She would have done anything for you."

"Except tell me the truth."

A long, heavy silence fell between them as the rescue workers worked to free Jack. If her father thought she was just going to forgive and forget, he was sorely mistaken.

Her father moved to stand in front of her, blocking her vision of Jack. Her father's worried gaze met hers. "We made a mistake. A big mistake. And we're sorry. Being a parent doesn't come with a guide book. We struggled, and we made the wrong decision, but it wasn't to hurt you. It was made because we love you."

She hated that there was a part of her that was so anxious to accept his apology and move on. The truth was that she never liked confrontations. She preferred to take the easy way out of tension-filled situations, which is partly why she'd gone into contract law. Courtroom battles seemed far too daunting for her.

And yet she couldn't just let her father off the hook. Not this time. She realized the enormity of the situation. Her father, the man she trusted most in the world, had lied to her for her entire life. That wasn't something that a simple apology could fix.

They were getting ready to lift the beam. And she wanted to be there for Jack.

She looked at her father once more. "No apology is going to mend this rift. And I can't do this now. I need to be with Jack."

For once her father didn't feel the need to have the final word as she stepped around him and walked away. She refused to glance back at him. She wouldn't give him that satisfaction.

Her heart felt as battered and torn as this room at the moment. She didn't know what would happen to her relationship with her father, and right now, she didn't have the spare energy to search for the answer.

Chapter Twenty-Three

Her sole focus was on Jack.

Lainey stood off to the side as the emergency crew warned him that there might be complications with his heart and his blood pressure when they lifted the beam. When they said his heart might stop, Lainey's breath hitched in the back of her throat. She sent up a silent prayer that he would be all right.

To her surprise, Jack seemed to be taking it all in stride. He was calm and composed, while she felt as though her stomach was twisted up into a million knots.

She wanted to be there by his side and hold his hand, but there were so many emergency workers surrounding him that there was no space for her. She hoped it wasn't an omen about their future.

"One. Two. Three."

Please let him be all right.

Time seemed to slow down.

The beam was carefully lifted. At last Jack was free.

Then the screech of an alarm sliced through the air.

Lainey's heart catapulted into her throat. *No. No. It couldn't be his heart.*

She struggled to see what was going on, but it was impossible. Between the darkness and the massive number of men rushing to his side, there was still no room for her.

She lifted up on her tiptoes, weaving and bobbing, trying to see Jack's face. *Somebody move.* As though they heard her thoughts, someone stepped aside, allowing her to see Jack.

The alarm was silenced, and she could at last see Jack's face. He was staring back at her and gave her a thumbs up.

The pent-up breath whished out of her lungs. A smile pulled at the corners of her lips as happy tears blurred her vision.

Now what?

The following afternoon, Jack kept asking himself that exact question. What was the next step for him and Lainey? He knew they needed to have a serious conversation before this thing between them got more serious, but it was never the right time.

She'd been by his side ever since his rescue. She'd insisted on staying with him at a Boston hospital, where he'd been transferred to from the Bluestar Medical Center. They'd poked and prodded him in every spot. There were so many tests. And in the end, he had a clean break in his leg that wouldn't require surgery as well as a bunch of bruises and cuts.

The whole time he'd been in the hospital, he'd tried to tell Lainey to go back to the island. She needed some proper rest, but she'd staunchly refused. Instead, she'd curled up in the chair next to his bed. She had promptly fallen asleep. He'd asked a nurse for an extra blanket to cover her up. He knew if the roles were reversed and it was Lainey in the hospital bed that he wouldn't have left her side either.

At last, they were back at his apartment. It was time for the dreaded conversation. He looked over at Lainey as she held Tux in her arms and hugged him. That cat was totally eating up the attention. Jack could hear the cat's purr clear across the room. He hated to tell his furry little buddy that he shouldn't get used to Lainey's company.

Jack slowly maneuvered himself to an armchair. He was still getting used to the crutches.

Lainey turned to him as Tux rubbed his head over her chin. "What can I get you?"

He shook his head. "I'm good. Why don't you come sit down?"

"I could go to the Lighthouse Café and get you some soup for later. Or maybe a pizza. Or I could get you both."

He'd noticed how she'd been antsy since she'd woken up in the hospital. Was it because she was trying to avoid dealing with the huge blow that had been dealt her yesterday when she learned the facts of her birth? Or was it because she realized the same thing he did? They didn't have a future together.

"Lainey, please sit."

She hesitated, but then she sat down on the end of the couch near him. Tux crawled out of her lap, only to sit down next to her and groom himself.

Jack struggled to start this conversation. He swallowed hard. "Thank you for staying with me at the hospital."

"I didn't really do much. I can't believe I fell asleep like that."

"You were exhausted both physically and mentally. You had a really big day."

Lainey hesitated and then nodded. "I'm still struggling with all of that. I think I will be for a long time. But I don't want to talk about that right now."

His gaze searched hers. "What do you want to talk about?"

His gut twisted into a painful knot. It was one thing to think about doing the right thing; it was totally different to follow through by actually doing the right thing. And the thought of saying goodbye to her had him hesitating.

"I think we should talk about us." She stared into his eyes. "I'm so sorry about you getting hurt."

He reached out to take her hand into his own but then realized he shouldn't do that. By touching her, it would muddle his thoughts and erode his resolve. He pulled back, resting his hand in his lap.

Instead he said, "We don't need to rehash that."

"Then what do we talk about?"

"The future."

She shook her head. "Jack, I can't. I don't know what I'm doing tomorrow much less next week."

"That's not it." The words stuck in the back of his throat. His heart told him not to do it, but his mind said this was for the best—for both of them. He cleared his throat, hoping when he spoke that his words would be clear. "I've given this a lot of thought and I...I think it would be best if we...if we stopped seeing each other."

He'd barely gotten the words out. He had no idea how painful they'd be. Each word spoken was like a new crack in his heart.

She gaped at him as her eyes shimmered with unshed tears. "You're dumping me."

"What? No. I just think with your life in New York City and... And I can't move there. I no longer have a job. Trying to make this thing"—he gestured between the two of them as he stumbled over the words—"that trying to make it work for the long term is too difficult. Eventually, we'd call it quits. If we keep this going, it'll hurt us more when we end things."

She shook her head. "No. This isn't happening. We are not breaking up."

He leaned forward. His every instinct was to reach out to her, and yet he couldn't allow himself that simple gesture. "Lainey, think about it. You're an attorney for your father's company. You're needed in the city. And my life, it's here on the island."

Her eyes widened like she'd just figured out a solution. "Come with me, and we'll find you a job in the city."

He shook his head. He knew he couldn't afford to move there without a good-paying job, and he wasn't going to take any handouts—not even from Lainey.

"You can't do this," Lainey pleaded.

"I'm not trying to hurt you. I'm really not."

"Well, you are because I love you."

Her words were a direct arrow to his heart. He didn't know how much he'd longed to hear those words until she'd spoken them. And yet he wouldn't let his aching heart take refuge in her admission. He was doing what was best for her.

He should say something, but he didn't trust his voice. His body was filled with conflicting emotions. If he said something in this moment, he wasn't sure what would come out of his mouth.

Her voice wobbled as she asked, "Don't you feel it?"

As she stared into his eyes with a desperation in her eyes, his resolve to do the right thing continued to crack. He realized he couldn't lie to her, even if it would make this easier.

He opened his mouth, and the words came rushing out. "I love you too."

A smile pulled at her lips as she moved to kneel in front of him. She peered up at him with tears still shimmering in her eyes. "I knew it."

When she lifted up on her knees to wrap her arms around him, he reached out and caught her arms before they could loop around his neck.

Confusion filled her eyes. "You love me. And I love you. We belong together."

He shook his head. "I can't hurt you any more than you've already been hurt by your family."

She pulled back. "Don't try to protect me. I can take care of myself."

"Maybe I'm trying to protect the both of us."

"Please, Jack, give us a chance. You don't know what the future will hold."

"I know what it's like when a loving relationship falls apart." His divorce had been so devastating in so many ways. "I don't want that for you."

"So, you're just going to push me away."

"You'll thank me one day."

"Don't do this." When he didn't respond, he noticed a hard glint in her eyes. "You're making the biggest mistake of your life."

He averted his gaze as he rubbed the back of his neck. He wished they weren't having this conversation in his apartment because if they were somewhere else, he could walk away. He could make this painful encounter as short as possible, not that it would ease the pain.

When he met her expectant gaze, he knew she was waiting for him to say something. "You're probably right."

"But you're going to do it anyway?" When he couldn't speak because the emotions were clogging his throat, and he feared if he spoke, he would take it all back, she said, "Fine. Have it your way." She got to her feet. "It's the accident. It shook you up, but you'll come to your senses, and I'll be waiting...just not too long."

Hadn't she heard a word he'd said? Had he said it all wrong? Probably. He shouldn't have admitted he loved her, but it was the truth.

Lainey walked away. A plea for her to come back hovered at the back of his throat, but he held it back. He wanted what was best for her. She would return to the city, and she would find someone that fit into her life. It just wouldn't be him. The thought pulled at the cracks in his heart.

Chapter Twenty-Four

WHAT HAD HE DONE?

As the sun sank lower in the sky long after Lainey had departed, Jack sat unmoving in the armchair. Their conversation had been so much worse than he'd ever imagined. His intention had been to save them both from getting hurt, but instead, they were both miserable.

Tux got up from his spot on the back of the couch. After yawning and stretching, he looked at Jack and lowered his ears. Then he turned his tail to Jack and headed for the bedroom. Even the cat knew he'd screwed up because Lainey was the best thing that had ever happened to him.

Jack kept telling himself that Lainey would get over it when she got back to her life in the city. A part of him wanted to believe it, but there was another part of him that knew you didn't always get over a loss. Was that the way it'd be for them?

Knock. Knock.

Lainey!

His heart hammered against his ribs. She realized he was totally out of his mind when he'd told her they were over. Thank goodness she hadn't believed a word he'd said, well, except for the part about him loving her. That was one hundred percent true.

She'd come back, and now he could tell her that he'd been out of his mind. Ending things was the absolute worst idea he'd ever had. Would she believe him?

He struggled to get to his feet. The crutches fell over. He reached for them, but they were out of his reach. Frustrated and anxious to get to the door—to Lainey—against the doctor's advice, he attempted to put weight on his injured leg. The piercing pain had him falling back into the chair as he bit back a yelp of pain.

Knock. Knock.

"Come in!"

The door creaked open. "Hello?"

The deep voice certainly didn't belong to Lainey, not unless she'd swallowed a toad. He craned his neck around. Lainey's father was headed toward him. His brows were drawn close together, and there were frown lines bracketing his mouth. The reason for his visit wasn't a good one.

"I'm having problems getting used to these crutches, so I can't get up."

"It's okay. Stay right there." The man took the seat that Lainey had just vacated. "How are you doing?"

Jack was taken aback by the man's friendly demeanor. He obviously hadn't heard about the mess of things he'd made with his daughter.

Glancing down at the cast on his leg, Jack said, "Not too bad. It was a clean break, so hopefully I won't need the cast for that long."

"I hope it heals quickly. I never got a chance to thank you for helping my daughter."

Jack shrugged off the words. "I don't know how much I helped her. It's more like it was the other way around."

"Not from the way I see it. My daughter was in that lighthouse all alone during a horrific storm. You went out there to make sure she was okay."

"And then I fell."

"Again, you saved her from the same fate because if you weren't the one on those steps, she would have been. So, I am in debt to you."

Jack shook his head. "You don't owe me anything."

"I had a feeling you would say that. It just makes me all the more certain about what I'm going to do."

Jack had absolutely no idea why this man was in his living room, throwing around compliments. Perhaps Jack should care, but after the way things ended with Lainey, he didn't have the energy.

"I appreciate what you said, but I'm not really up for company now." He would just let the man think his reluctance for company had something to do with his injury.

"I understand." Mr. Devereaux pulled a white envelope from his suit jacket. "I have an offer for you."

This got Jack's attention. What sort of offer was he going to make? Was he going to pay him off to stay away from his daughter? He was too late. "Listen, sir, if this is about your daughter, um, things are over between us."

He noticed the slight widening of Mr. Devereaux's eyes. It happened so fast that if Jack had blinked, he would have missed it.

"This offer has nothing to do with your relationship with my daughter."

"I don't understand. Then what are you doing here?"

"I've been reconsidering my company's goals. I now believe that we are letting valuable assets slip through our fingers."

Jack still didn't know what the man was going on about. "What assets?"

"You for one."

"Me?"

Mr. Devereaux nodded. "And the rest of your team. I want you to come work for me."

Jack shook his head. "This was Lainey's idea, wasn't it?"

"Lainey?"

"Yes. She just left here. Did she go to you and ask you to make this job offer?"

"No. I don't consult my daughter on who I hire. In fact, I haven't seen her since yesterday. Right now, I don't know if she'll ever speak to me again." The anguish threaded through his voice as the pain shone in his eyes.

The man had a point; Lainey was furious with her father. She didn't think there was anything that would cause her to go to him and ask a favor. This left Jack not knowing what to make of this offer.

"Just think about it." The man got to his feet and handed him the white envelope. Then the man picked up Jack's fallen crutches and handed them to him. "I'll see myself out."

After the door closed behind Mr. Devereaux, Jack slipped his finger through the flap of the envelope and ripped it open. He pulled out the folded papers to find that it was a job offer. He skipped to the end to find a very generous salary offer and a notation that said he was planning to hire the rest of Jack's team.

Jack couldn't believe what he was reading. It was too good to be true. He read it again. The offer sounded even better the second time around. What was he supposed to do now?

She never should have come to Bluestar Island.

The next morning started the Spring Fling celebration. The whole island was abuzz except for Lainey. She sat at a table in the Lighthouse Café, sipping a cup of coffee. She didn't have an appetite.

Lainey couldn't stop replaying the scene with Jack. How could he have told her he loved her in one breath and in the next said they were over?

She wanted to march over to his apartment and tell him he was passing up the best thing he would ever have in his life. Instead, she sat there, sipping her coffee while watching people rush in for a quick bite to eat before they returned to the festivities of the Spring Fling.

She noticed a young girl with her mother. The girl was busy chatting away about something. There was no break in her words, so the mother was left to nod here and there. It reminded Lainey of her and her mother. Oh, how she missed those days. Back then, life seemed so simple.

"Lainey?"

She glanced up to see Maude standing there. The woman looked better than she had the other night. There was color in her cheeks and light in her eyes.

Lainey felt a smile pull at the corners of her lips. If anyone understood how she felt it was Maude because they'd both been blindsided by her mother's deception. "Hi. Would you like to join me?"

Maude hesitated. "I don't have long. I'm supposed to help with the egg decorating contest. But I have a few minutes." She smiled as she sat down. "I was hoping we would get to speak again."

Guilt settled on Lainey. "I'm sorry I disappeared. A lot has happened."

"And I heard about your experience at the lighthouse. Are you all right?"

"I'm fine, but how did you hear?"

"One thing you'll learn quickly about this island is that it has a healthy and rapid gossip chain. There's nothing that happens on this island that everyone else doesn't know."

"Oh. Wow. So does everyone know about you and me?" She wasn't sure she was ready for that. She hadn't come to terms with it herself.

"Surprisingly no. I haven't told anyone. Like you, I'm still adjusting to the news. Though selfishly I am thrilled to have you in my life."

"You are?" Lainey had been so caught up in how this news affected her that she hadn't thought of how Maude would feel about it.

Maude smiled and nodded. "How could I not be?" She leaned forward and lowered her voice to a whisper. "You're an amazing young woman, and I'm so anxious to get to know you better. And I'm proud to call you my granddaughter." The smile slipped from her face. "I'm sorry. I should have asked you if it's all right to call you that."

Lainey's childhood wish to have a grandparent came rushing back to her. "I would like that. But I'm not ready to go public just yet."

Maude reached across the table and patted her hand. "I understand. And I'm around any time you want to talk. Stop by the house whenever you want. I'm usually around. And I'll pull out some pictures for you to look at."

"I would like that." Lainey blinked back the tears of happiness. In the darkness of deceit, there was a silver lining, and her name was Maude. "Thank you."

"I need to get going. I don't want to be late for the egg decorating. I'm one of the judges this year. I don't want them to think I don't take my responsibilities seriously." She moved to get up. "You and Jack are running the three-legged race, aren't you?"

She nodded. "Except Jack isn't going to be able to help me since he broke his leg."

She would coordinate the races on her own. It wouldn't be easy but doable. It wasn't like she knew that many people on the island and certainly no one she would impose upon to help her.

"Maybe he'll surprise you." Maude stood. "It's all going to work out. Sometimes it just takes a little time."

And then Maude was gone. Lainey was left wondering if the woman was referring to the news of her birth or the way things had ended with Jack. Was it possible Maude knew Jack had broken up with her?

Impossible. She hadn't told anyone. Would Jack have talked about it? She doubted it. He wasn't exactly the most forthcoming with his emotions.

She didn't have time to think about it any longer. She needed to get to the park and start setting up the area for the three-legged race.

The supplies were at the community center. She'd borrowed a cart from the inn. With her on her own, she was going to need all the help she could get.

She thought of the poster at Jack's place. *Nope.* She wasn't going there, even if the thought of seeing him again tempted and teased her mind. *Nope.* Wasn't going to happen. She could just make another sign. It wouldn't be pretty like the other one that had glittery Easter eggs and two rabbits doing a three-legged race, but she'd just make do.

It took her longer than she thought to get to the community center. The streets were busy with carts and bikes alike. The sidewalks were filled with residents with smiles on their faces as they set off to enjoy the many events.

At last, Lainey made it to the back of the community center. She stepped inside where Ethan Walker and Kent Turner gathered the cones, white spray paint, posts, and yellow tape before placing them in the back of her cart.

"Do you have a tape measure?" Ethan asked.

"Uh. No." She couldn't help but wonder what else she'd forgotten. She was sure if Jack was with her that he'd have been all over these details.

Buzz-buzz.

It wasn't her phone. As soon as she realized it wasn't her phone—Jack wasn't trying to reach her—disappointment assailed her.

She'd hoped he would have called her by now. She didn't know what to say to him to change his mind about them. If Jack wasn't brave enough to take a chance on them, maybe it really wouldn't have worked out anyway. This realization did nothing to bolster her.

Kent pulled out his phone. "I've got to get this."

After Kent stepped outside, Ethan said, "Here. You can use this tape measure." He hesitated after he'd handed her it. "Do you need some help setting things up?"

She shook her head. "I can do it. There's not much to do."

She kept wishing Jack was there with her. It would have made this day fun. As it was, she was just going through the motions.

Ethan walked her out to the cart. "I feel really bad about this."

"Don't. I've got this." She glanced around for Kent. She wanted to thank him again for giving her the job at the furniture shop and helping her out during a difficult period because in the next day or two, she was leaving the island. "Do you know where Kent went?"

Ethan glanced around. "I have no idea."

That was strange. He'd said he was taking a phone call, and then he just disappeared. *Oh well.* Hopefully, she'd run into him sometime during that day.

There was someone else she longed to see that day. Jack. She doubted that would happen with his broken leg. She didn't think he'd be up for going to the festival on crutches.

Thankfully, she had a lot to keep her busy instead of letting her mind wallow in the way things had ended with Jack. She would be busy measuring out the area for the three-legged race.

She easily found the spot for the race. Using tall stakes and orange cones, she taped off the area with bright yellow warning tape. A few people that meandered past asked her what she was setting up. She told them. Too bad she didn't have the sign for the race that she'd made with Jack.

The sound of a cart approaching had her turning. She saw Kent, and a smile pulled at her lips. It would be nice to have a friend around. But then she noticed he wasn't alone.

Wait. Is that Jack in the passenger seat?

As they drew nearer, her suspicion was confirmed. Jack was sitting there, staring back at her. Her heart pitter-pattered. *What is he doing here?*

Chapter Twenty-Five

Was it possible he'd come to his senses?

Lainey's palms grew damp. She knew she shouldn't stand there, staring. Did she really want to be obvious that his presence meant something to her? But her feet refused to move.

The cart pulled to a stop in front of her. Kent jumped out. "We thought you might need some help. Right, Jack?"

Jack was staring at her, continuing to make her heart pitter-patter. He nodded his head. "We're here to help."

She swallowed hard, unable to stop staring into his eyes. "I... I have most of it set up."

Jack struggled to reach the crutches in the back of the cart. She rushed over and retrieved them for him. She handed them to him. When his fingers brushed over hers, a spark of electricity made her hand tingle. His fingers tightened over hers. The stirring sensation raced up her arm and set her heart pounding.

Her gaze strayed to his lips. What would he do if she was to lean over and press her lips to his?

Would he pull her closer? Her body started to sway forward.

She caught herself just in time and pulled back. She couldn't think straight. Yanking her hand from his, she stepped away.

What was she doing here? She'd already had her heart yanked out and ripped apart. She wasn't up for a repeat.

"Jack, you don't have to be here," she said. "I can handle this on my own."

Kent walked over to join them. His gaze moved between the two of them as they stared at each other. He cleared his throat. "We knew you needed a sign. Isn't that right, Jack?"

"Uh..." Jack glanced off to the side and then back at her. "Yes. That's right." He gestured with his hand. "Is that where you want the sign?"

"Anywhere is fine." She didn't want to turn away. She wanted to keep talking to him. She'd missed the sound of his voice.

"I really think you should look at it."

She didn't know why he was making such a big deal out of the sign. If it would make him happy, she'd check it out. People just needed to know this was the spot for the race.

However, when she turned around and her gaze settled on the sign, the breath caught in her throat. This was not the sign she'd made with Jack. It was the same size and just as colorful and glittery, but it was the message that had tears blurring her vision.

The sign read:
Lainey, I'm so sorry.
Please forgive me.
I love you, Jack

She blinked repeatedly, trying to hold back the tears. She read the sign again just to make sure she hadn't misread it.

Then she turned a questioning gaze to him. She was afraid to put herself out there, only to be hurt again.

Jack leaned on his crutches as he reached out his hand to her. As if her arm acted of its own volition, she reached out to him, too, placing her hand in his. Another electrical charge jolted her racing heart.

She wanted to tell him she loved him, too, but she was still hesitant. Her job was in the city, and she wasn't sure she was ready to give up on it. Could they make a long-distance relationship work?

Her gaze settled on Jack. She wanted to build something with Jack, but she had to be certain it was what he wanted too.

"Jack, why did you do this?" Her gaze searched his.

"Because I made the biggest mistake of my life last night. I wasn't ready to trust in our love. I was afraid to believe that our love could see us through the good times and the bad."

"And you're ready to do that now?" The breath hitched in her throat as she waited for his answer.

He nodded. "I am. I have to admit that your father helped me see the light."

Her pent-up breath rushed out. She didn't like the thought of her father going behind her back and speaking to Jack. If her father thought he was going to use Jack to help fix their relationship, he was clearly mistaken. "My father? What did he say to you?"

"Stop looking so worried. We had a nice conversation. Actually, he did most of the talking. In the end, he offered me a job—well, actually he offered my whole team a job working for his company."

"Wait. You're going to work for my father?" She wasn't sure how she felt about that. Things were still so tangled and twisted with her father.

"I don't know. I haven't made up my mind. I thought maybe you and I could talk it over. But it made me think that if I could get a job with your father's company, why couldn't I get another job in the city? I know I've only worked for one company since I graduated college, and my resume isn't up to date, but I'm willing to do whatever it takes to make us work."

Her heart swelled with love. "You're willing to move away from this island and your family so that we can be together?"

He nodded his head. "I would follow you to the moon if that's what it took for us to be together. I love you, Lainey. And I can't imagine my life without you in it."

She stepped closer to him. She withdrew her hands from his hold in order to loop them around his neck. She stared deep into his eyes. "I love you too. I don't know what the future holds for us, but as long as we're together, I believe it'll all work out."

"I do too."

A warmth swirled in her chest and filled her heart. His love filled in the cracks in her heart, making it whole once more. She lifted up on her tiptoes and pressed her lips to his. No other kiss had ever felt so right.

Someone cleared their throat. Lainey jerked out of his arms to find them surrounded by Bluestar residents all smiling at them. A round of applause filled the air.

Her cheeks grew warm. She had a feeling it was going to take her a bit to get used to this small-town living—even if it was only part-time.

Jack took her hand in his and gave it a squeeze. He leaned over to her and said, "I think they approve."

She turned her head to him. "I think you're right."

She leaned forward and pressed a quick kiss to his lips. "I love you."

"I love you too."

"Hey," Grant said, "isn't there supposed to be a three-legged race?"

The heat returned to Lainey's cheeks. "Yes, there is."

She insisted that Jack rest. He sat in the golf cart and kept his leg elevated. Kent volunteered to help her run the races.

She was able to push aside the pain she felt over learning the circumstances of her birth and instead focus on the moment. There was a lot of laughter. How could there not be when watching a three-legged race?

Chapter Twenty-Six

She couldn't stop smiling.

This day was really looking up.

Lainey had so much fun overseeing the three-legged race. She was able to let go of her troubles and just enjoy the moment with a lot of friendly people and the man she loved nearby. It felt like she finally made it through the darkness in her life, and the sun was starting to shine through the clouds.

When the race was over, Jack's brothers Kent and Grant insisted on cleaning up. Lainey wasn't about to argue with them. She was a little tired after all that had happened the past few days plus her inability to fall asleep the night before.

She made her way over to Jack, who was scrolling on his phone. "How do you think it went?"

He turned his phone around to show her what he was looking at. He'd snapped photos of her laughing and others of his brothers smiling. There were some snapshots of Bluestar residents racing to the finish line.

She looked over at him. "Since when did you take up photography?"

"I just thought you'd want something to remember this day."

"Thank you." A smile pulled at the corner of her lips. "I don't think I'll ever forget this day."

"Me either."

She was just about to lean over and give Jack a kiss when her father approached them. "Elaine."

She turned to her father. The smile fled from her face. "I'm not ready to talk."

There were dark circles under her father's eyes. She'd never noticed that before. Her mother used to say nothing could keep her father awake. It looked like that wasn't the case anymore.

Lainey wanted to summon some sympathy for him, but in this case, she couldn't do it. He'd brought this on himself with the lies he'd helped her mother perpetuate. It wasn't like she was sleeping that well either.

"I'm sorry things worked out like this. I was wrong, and if I could go back and change things, I would. But I'll never regret having you as a daughter, even if it meant you came into this world in an unusual way. I just wanted you to have this." He handed her a white envelope. "I love you with all of my heart. I hope one day you'll be able to forgive me." He cleared his throat. "I'm leaving the island, and I won't be back." Without another word, her father turned and walked off.

Was there a slight droop to his broad shoulders? No. She wasn't going to feel bad for him. Not this time.

Jack's gaze moved to the white envelope and then back to her. "Do you think you got a job offer too?"

She looked at the envelope. There was no hint of what might be inside. And though it killed her, she was curious. What would her father find important enough to write down in the aftermath of her learning the truth about herself—about her mothers.

"You know you want to read it," Jack said softly. "Why don't you go to the seawall and see what he has to say? I need to stay here and boss my brothers around, or they'll never get done cleaning things up."

She hesitated. Did she want to know what her father had to say? Would it make things better? Or worse?

Jack gave her a gentle nudge. "If you don't read it, it'll nag at you the rest of the day."

He was right. Jack was good at looking out for her. And so with reluctance, she took his advice and went to sit on the wall.

Lainey took a deep breath, trying to calm her racing pulse. She wondered what her father thought was so important that he'd given her this envelope with no explanation.

Her father wasn't one to be cryptic. He believed in being straightforward and to the point. And then she thought of the lie he'd been hiding her whole life. Maybe he wasn't so straightforward after all.

She hated how it felt as though the rug had been pulled out from under her. A year ago, she would have sworn she had the most solid family. She had never been so wrong.

She looked at the envelope. She shouldn't even bother reading it. It didn't matter what her father said; she wasn't going to forgive him. At least not today.

And yet there was a voice in the back of her head, prodding her to open it. There might be some more information to glean about her mother's choices.

Her fingers dug under the glued flap on the envelope and pulled. She withdrew the folded paper. She noticed the slight tremble in her hands. She unfolded the papers and was surprised to see that it was her mother's distinctive handwriting.

My dearest Elaine,

I knew this day would come. Was it wrong of me to wish you never found out the truth? That you could have stayed my sweet baby forever?

The truth is that I attempted to tell you the truth on numerous occasions, but I could never utter the words. I always lost my courage. I was so worried about losing your love.

I wanted you so much. Please believe that. I had a meltdown when I found out I was infertile. I went off on a road trip. I had a lot to think about. But no matter how many miles I drove, I couldn't give up on the thought of you.

Lainey paused to wipe the tears from her eyes. She missed her mother so much that it hurt. Even though her mother had kept all of this from her, she still loved her...just like she loved her father. It didn't mean she wasn't angry with both of them, but this letter had broken through her protective shell and let the glimmer of love shine through.

She turned her attention back to her mother's words...

My cousin Louise, who was more like a sister, donated her egg in order to make my dream of having a baby come true. The dream didn't come without its sacrifices, but I would have done anything for you to be a part of my life. Please never doubt your father's and my love for you.

If you are reading this, it means I'm no longer able to tell you all of this in person. I'm so sorry. But always know that I am there with you, watching over you and cheering you on. You can be anything you want to be. You just have to believe in yourself.

I love you,
Mom

There was a drop that landed on the page, smudging the blue ink. She glanced up. The sky was clear blue. It wasn't rain. She reached up and touched her cheek. It was damp with tears.

Her heart ached. This was what her mother had been trying to tell her at the end. Lainey inwardly groaned. She hated the fact that her mother wasn't here so they could yell it out, and she would like to think they would eventually have hugged it out. That was what made this whole situation so much worse.

"Hey. How are you doing?" Jack took a seat next to her on the wall.

She swiped at her cheeks. "I think that in the end, my mother's secret was a blessing."

"A blessing? How's that?"

"Well, it brought me to this magical island. And even though I permanently lost some of my memory, I found the coolest lighthouse, a grandmother that I never thought I would have, and I met the man of my dreams." She stared deeply into his eyes. "I love you."

"I love you too." He leaned over and gave her the most gentle, sensuous kiss. She felt it clear down to the tips of her toes. If she'd had any doubt about his feelings for her, she didn't now. The warmth of his love flowed through his kiss straight to her heart.

When he pulled back, he softly asked, "Are you ready to forgive your father?"

"No. Not yet. But my mother used to tell me that time has a way of healing. I guess I'm about to find out if she's right."

Jack wrapped his arm over her shoulder and drew her close to his side. She leaned her head against him. For a moment, they sat together in silence. Lainey watched the sunshine dance upon the water. She wasn't sure where things would go from here, but with Jack by her side, they'd muddle through it all together.

"Are you ready to go back to the festival?" Jack asked.

"Maybe we should get you home so you can rest your leg."

"Any chance I can talk you into pizza and a movie?"

"I think there's a very good chance I'll take you up on that offer."

"That's good because Tux has been mad at me since you left yesterday."

"Mad at you?"

"Mm-hm. He won't sit with me. He doesn't like anything I feed him. I think he's on strike."

As they made their way back across the street to the park, there were a lot of people having picnics. She liked to think that one of these days, she and Jack would be one of those couples with their own family.

"Dr. Grant, help!" a voice in the crowd called. "There's been an accident."

"That doesn't sound good," Jack said as he tried to pick up the pace on his crutches.

"Slow down before you fall. Your big brother can handle it."

Join Dr. Grant Turner as he comes to the aid of Paige Maxwell, the long-lost great niece of Horace Blackwell in INHERITING HER ISLAND HOUSE. Eccentric Uncle Horace has a few unusual stipulations in order for Paige to inherit his entire estate, and she has some stipulations of her own where Grant is concerned. It's going to be a summer of adjustments for these two. Maybe they will find a way to help each other...

Epilogue

Christmas, Bluestar Island

After being gone for a couple of months, Lainey was so happy to be back on the island. This would be her first Christmas in Bluestar. She hoped it would be the first of many.

Jack's parents had invited them plus her grandmother and her father for the holidays. Her father had readily accepted the invitation before she even knew he was invited. She wasn't sure how she felt about it.

Over the past eight months, she'd returned to work for the family company while she decided what career path she wanted to follow. And at the beginning of December, she'd turned in her notice. Come the New Year, she would be able to follow her passion—photography and writing books about the history of places throughout the States.

Even though this new adventure would give her the ability to travel, her home base was still in Manhattan. Jack lived there now that he'd taken her father up on the job offer. In the beginning, she wasn't sure how Jack would do living so far from the island and his family, but he was happy and thriving at the company.

They came back to the island as much as their schedules would allow, which wasn't nearly often enough for her. So, it was really nice to be here for the holidays.

"It's so good to have you here," Jack's mother said as she stood next to her at the tree lighting.

"Thank you for inviting us." Lainey gazed up at the tree as its white lights twinkled in the evening sky.

"No need to thank me. You're like family now." The warm smile on the woman's face said she meant every word.

She loved Jack's big family. They could be loud and a bit chaotic at times, but the love that ran through the family was always evident. And they were always there for each other.

Lainey glanced around for Jack. She finally spotted him speaking to her father. More and more, she found them with their heads together. She didn't know how she felt about their budding relationship when she was still struggling to find her footing with her father. She knew it would take time for her to make peace with him. She also knew they would never have the easy, close relationship they'd experienced in the past. Change was a part of life, but that didn't make it any easier. But at least she could be in the same room with him and make small talk.

With the Christmas tree reveal over, the crowd started to drift away. Jack made his way over to her. When his gaze met hers, her heart pitter-pattered just like it always did. A smile pulled at the corners of her lips.

"Did you enjoy the unveiling?" His voice was warm and wrapped around her like a hug.

"I did. The tree is beautiful."

"Not as beautiful as you."

Her heart fluttered. "You always know the right things to say to make this girl feel special."

"Then you might like what I have to say next."

Curiosity consumed her. "What are you up to?"

He took her by the hand and led her closer to the lit Christmas tree. He stopped and turned to her. Before she could ask more questions, he pulled something from his pocket and then dropped to his knee.

Lainey gasped. Was he proposing? He opened a black velvet box, and a diamond ring sparkled beneath the tree's twinkle lights.

Her heart pitter-pattered. Was this really happening? They were going to make this most amazing relationship official. She couldn't think of anything she'd like more than to be Jack's wife, for now and always.

He gazed up at her. "Lainey, I knew the first time you opened your eyes and stared into mine that there was something special about you. You showed me that it was all right to open my heart and love again. You believed in me, even when I didn't believe in myself. I don't know where our life's journey will lead us, but as long as we're together, everything will work out."

She swiped at her cheeks as happy tears streamed down them. In that moment, it felt as though the world had melted away, and it was just the two of them. She'd never been happier in her life.

He pulled the diamond solitaire from the box and took her hand. "Elaine Devereaux, I love you with all of my heart. Will you marry me?"

The words came rushing out of her mouth. "I will."

He slid the ring onto her finger. She had a feeling he'd done a bit of sleuthing to get just the right size. How had she not seen this coming?

Maybe because things had been so traumatic since her mother's death that when things settled down for the both of them in New York, she'd just appreciated the peace.

She wished her mother could have been here to see her get her happily ever after. The twinkle of a brilliant star caught her eye. Maybe that was her mother sending her a message that she was there with her. The thought comforted her.

Jack straightened. He pulled her into his embrace. His gaze met hers. "I love you."

"I love you too."

And then his head lowered. His lips caught hers. And all around them there was a roar of applause. Happy tears slipped down her cheeks once more.

When they parted, she leaned close to him. "Do you think we could have a house here on the island?"

"I think that's definitely something we can work on."

Before she could say more, people rushed up to congratulate them. While Jack's mother hugged him, Lainey's father stepped up to her. His gaze shimmered in the glow of the Christmas tree. Were those tears in his eyes?

Her father blinked. "I'm so happy for you. And so, when he asked for your hand..."

"Jack asked for your blessing?" She had no idea Jack could be such a traditionalist. She wondered what else she didn't know about her future husband. She couldn't wait to find out. Life was not boring with him in it.

Her father nodded his head. "Jack is a good man, and I don't say that lightly. You know it would take someone special to gain my approval—not that you need it. I hope you and he have an amazing love story like your mother and I had. I miss her every day. But it's at times like this when I feel her all around us. I think she would have approved of this marriage too. Be good to each other."

She sniffed as the waterworks started again. This was the first lengthy conversation she had with her father since she'd learned the truth about her birth. "We will."

And then she leaned forward and hugged her dad. He held her close. This time it was he who was doing the sniffling. Maybe things were starting to improve. Little by little.

When her father moved aside, her grandmother was the next in line to congratulate her. Maude rushed up to Lainey and hugged her tightly.

When Maude pulled back, she said, "I have an early wedding gift for you."

"You do?" She couldn't imagine what her grandmother wanted to give her.

Maude nodded. She opened her big handbag and pulled out some folded papers. She handed them over. "This is the deed to the lighthouse. I want you to have it, and if you have children, you can hand it down to them."

"Oh, Maude. Thank you." Again, the happy tears started. She couldn't remember the last time she'd cried so much. "I will take good care of it."

"I know you will, sweetie. That's why I'm giving it to you."

After more hugs and congratulations, Jack was back by her side. They opted to walk back to his parents' house, where they were staying for the holidays. They wanted a little alone time to talk and take in the moment.

As they walked, she told him about the deed to the lighthouse. Jack was surprised and suggested the first thing they do is repair all of the steps. She readily agreed.

As big fluffy snowflakes started to fall, they stopped and turned to each other. With their arms around each other, they both said, "I love you," in unison.

Keep reading Lainey and Jack's story! Sign up for my newsletter and receive a Bonus Epilogue.

Get your bonus epilogue HERE.

The Elegant Bakery's Whoopie Pies

3 cups flour
1 tsp baking soda
2 tsp unsweetened cocoa powder
1 ½ cups oil
1 tsp white vinegar
One small bottle red food coloring
1 tsp vanilla
1 ½ cups sugar
2 eggs
1 cup buttermilk

Filling:
5 Tbsp flour
1 cup milk
1 cup sugar
8 Tbsp butter, softened
½ cup vegetable shortening
2 tsp vanilla

To make cakes:
- Preheat 350°.

- Lightly grease cookie sheets.

- Blend ingredients.

- Drop batter by tablespoon on sheets, leave a couple inches between batter.

- Bake until domes of cake are firm, about 12 mins. Cool completely.

To make filling:
- Put flour in pan and whisk in milk.

- Over medium heat, stirring constantly until thick, about 3 minutes.

- Allow to cool completely.

- Cream sugar, butter, shortening, and vanilla with mixer.

- Add the cooled flour mixture and whip until fluffy.

- Spread on half of the cakes and top with a plain cake.

- Individually wrap each whoopie pie in plastic wrap and refrigerate.

- Enjoy!

Afterword

Thanks so much for reading Lainey and Jack's story. I hope their journey made your heart smile. If you did enjoy the book, please consider...

- Help spreading the word about A Lighthouse Snapshot by writing a review.
- Subscribe to my newsletter in order to receive information about my next release as well as find out about giveaways and special sales.
- You can like my author page on Facebook or follow me on Twitter.

I hope you'll come back to Bluestar Island and read the continuing adventures of its residents. In upcoming books, there will be updates on Lainey and Jack as well as the addition of some new islanders.

Coming next is Brianna and Grant's story in Inheriting Her Island House.

Thanks again for your support! It is HUGELY appreciated.

Happy reading,
Jennifer

About Author

Award-winning author, Jennifer Faye pens fun, heartwarming contemporary romances. With more than a million books sold, she is internationally published with books translated into more than a dozen languages and her work has been optioned for film. She is a two-time winner of the RT Book Reviews Reviewers' Choice Award, the CataRomance Reviewers' Choice Award, named a TOP PICK author, and been nominated for numerous other awards.

Now living her dream, she resides with her very patient husband and two spoiled cats. When she's not plotting out her next romance, you can find her curled up with a mug of tea and a book. You can learn more about Jennifer at www.Jennifer-Faye.com

Subscribe to Jennifer's newsletter for news about upcoming releases, bonus content and other special offers.

You can also join her on Twitter, Facebook, or Goodreads.

Also By

Other titles available by Jennifer Faye include:

BLUESTAR ISLAND:

Love Blooms

Harvest Dance

A Lighthouse Café Christmas

Rising Star

Summer by the Beach

Brass Anchor Inn

Summer Refresh

A Seaside Bookshop Christmas
A Lighthouse Snapshot
Inheriting Her Island House

SEABREEZE WEDDING CHAPEL:

The Bride's Dream Wedding

The Bride's Pink Shoes

The Bride's Christmas Dress

The Runaway Bride's Vow
The Bride's Antique Ring

WHISTLE STOP ROMANCE SERIES:

A Moment to Love

A Moment to Dance

A Moment on the Lips

A Moment to Cherish

A Moment at Christmas

TANGLED CHARMS:

Sprinkled with Love

A Mistletoe Kiss

GREEK PARADISE ESCAPE:

Greek Heir to Claim Her Heart

It Started with a Royal Kiss

Second Chance with the Bridesmaid

WEDDING BELLS IN LAKE COMO:

Bound by a Ring & a Secret

Falling for Her Convenient Groom

ONCE UPON A FAIRYTALE:

Beauty & Her Boss

Miss White & the Seventh Heir

Fairytale Christmas with the Millionaire

THE BARTOLINI LEGACY:

The Prince and the Wedding Planner

The CEO, the Puppy & Me

The Italian's Unexpected Heir

GREEK ISLAND BRIDES:

Carrying the Greek Tycoon's Baby

Claiming the Drakos Heir

Wearing the Greek Millionaire's Ring

Click here to find all of Jennifer's titles and buy links.

Made in the USA
Las Vegas, NV
20 July 2024